Having Sam around was a distraction.

He didn't look like the man who had battered her young heart—and a good portion of her soul—eight years ago when she'd been twenty, but he was the same type. That outrageous masculinity, the untamed don't-give-a-damn look that sang to something wild and feminine and reckless in her. A part of herself she thought she'd long suppressed.

Panic started its heart-stopping, breath-stealing, muscle-tensing attack on her. She took in a deep breath that came out halfway to a sob.

'You okay?' Sam's deep voice was warm with concern.

She pretended to cough. 'F…Fine, thanks,' she said. 'Just…just a tickle in my throat.'

She dropped her hand from his shoulder, stepped away so his hand fell from her waist.

And immediately felt bereft of his touch.

Dear Reader

In this, my second book for Mills & Boon, I'm thrilled to take you back to the small coastal town of Dolphin Bay on the idyllic south coast of New South Wales, Australia. While the town is fictional, the charming harbour and beautiful unspoiled beaches are inspired by places I have visited and loved.

Kate Parker was a character in my previous book, THE SUMMER THEY NEVER FORGOT. I liked Kate a lot and wanted her to have a book of her own. Kate delights in helping people, and in THE TYCOON AND THE WEDDING PLANNER she's in her element, organising a very special wedding.

Romance is in the air when Kate meets gorgeous Sam Lancaster. But Kate is hiding secrets from the past that threaten her chance of happiness with Sam—and he has some secrets of his own.

I so enjoyed unravelling the defences Kate and Sam put up against the love they both deserve—I hope you will enjoy reading their story.

Kandy

THE TYCOON
AND THE
WEDDING PLANNER

BY
KANDY SHEPHERD

First published in Great Britain 2014
by Mills & Boon, an imprint of Harlequin (UK) Limited,
Eton House, 18-24 Paradise Road, Richmond, Surrey, TW9 1SR

© 2014 Kandy Shepherd

ISBN: 978 0 263 24265 2

Harlequin (UK) Limited's policy is to use papers that are natural,
renewable and recyclable products and made from wood grown in
sustainable forests. The logging and manufacturing processes conform
to the legal environmental regulations of the country of origin.

Printed and bound in Great Britain
by CPI Antony Rowe, Chippenham, Wiltshire

Kandy Shepherd swapped a fast-paced career as a magazine editor for a life writing romance. She lives on a small farm in the Blue Mountains near Sydney, Australia, with her husband, daughter, and a menagerie of animal friends. Kandy believes in love at first sight and real-life romance—they worked for her!

Kandy loves to hear from her readers. Visit her website at: www.kandyshepherd.com

Recent titles by Kandy Shepherd:

THE SUMMER THEY NEVER FORGOT

**This and other titles by Kandy Shepherd
are also available in eBook format
from www.millsandboon.co.uk**

To my wonderful husband and daughter
for your love and inspiration—thank you!

CHAPTER ONE

As SHE WENT about her lunchtime front-of-house duties at the Hotel Harbourside restaurant, Kate Parker was only too aware of the ill-concealed interest in her. The too-interested glances quickly averted; the undertones; the murmurs.

Poor Kate.

If she heard—or sensed—that phrase one more time, she'd scream.

Her and her big, big mouth.

Why, oh, why had she made such a big deal of her childhood crush on Jesse Morgan? She wished she'd never told a soul, let alone all and sundry in her home town of Dolphin Bay, that the next time Jesse was back she'd finally let him know how she really felt about him.

Because now he was home, now she had kissed him for the first time since they'd been just kids fifteen years ago, and it had turned out a total disaster. She'd felt nothing. *Absolutely nothing.* Instead of turning her on, his kiss had turned her off. She'd fought the urge to wipe her mouth with the back of her hand.

And Jesse? He'd been as embarrassed and awkward as she'd been. They'd parted, barely able to look each other in the eye.

She cringed at the memory—as she'd cringed a hundred times already—as painfully fresh today as it had been three days ago when it had occurred.

And now everyone in their small community knew she'd made an utter fool of herself by believing there could be anything more between her and Jesse than the affection due to a family friend she'd known since they'd both been in nappies.

Poor Kate.

The air was thick with pity for her. She looked around the restaurant; many of the tables were already full for Sunday lunch.

She wanted to run out the door, down the steps onto the beach below and get home to lock herself in her bedroom with the music turned up loud.

Instead, she girded herself against the gossip. She forced herself to smile. First, because a warm, confident smile was essential to any role in hospitality. And second, because she couldn't bear for any of those too-interested townsfolk to guess how churned up, anxious and panicky she was feeling inside.

It meant nothing, people, she wanted to broadcast to the room in general. *Less than nothing. I walked away from that darn kiss completely unaffected.*

But that wouldn't be completely true.

Because the Great Kiss Disaster had left her doubting everything she'd believed about who was the right man for her. She'd discovered the man she'd thought was Mr Perfect was not, in fact. So where did she go next? How could she ever trust her judgement of men again?

Smile. Smile. Smile.

The restaurant in the award-winning hotel was one of the best places to eat in Dolphin Bay. More people were arriving for lunch. She had a job she valued. She wanted to be promoted to hotel manager and she wouldn't achieve that by moping around feeling sorry for herself.

She took a deep, steadying breath, forced her lips to curve upwards in a big welcome and aimed it at the next customer—a man who had pushed his way through the glass doors that led from the steps from the beach and into the restaurant.

She nearly dropped the bottle of wine she was holding with hands that had gone suddenly nerveless. He caught her smile and nodded in acknowledgement.

Where the heck had he *come from?*

She'd never seen him in Dolphin Bay before, that was for sure.

Dark-haired, tall and powerfully built, his broad shoulders and muscular arms strained against his black T-shirt, his hard thighs against the worn denim of his jeans. His heavy black boots were hardly seaside resort wear, but they worked. Boy, did they work.

No wonder the two young waitresses on duty stampeded past her to show him to the best table in the house. She had to hold herself back from pulling rank and elbowing them out of the way to get to him first.

His stance was easy, confident, as he waited to be shown to a table. Her heart started to pound double-quick time. When had she last felt the kind of awareness of a man that made her ache for him to notice her?

But, when his gaze did turn in her direction, she quickly ducked her head and studiously read the label on the wine bottle without registering a single word.

She looked up again to see the young waitress who had won the race to get to him first looking up at him in open admiration and laughing at something he'd said. Did the guy realise half the female heads in the room had swivelled to attention when he'd strode in?

Not that he looked like he cared much about what people thought. His dark brown hair was several months away from a haircut—shoved back off his face with his fingers rather than a comb, by the look of it. The dark growth on his jaw was halfway to a beard.

He looked untamed. Sexy. And dangerous.

Way too dangerous.

She was shocked by the powerful punch of attraction that slammed her, the kind of visceral pull that had caused her such terrible hurt in the past. That was so different from how she'd felt for safe, familiar Jesse. She never wanted to feel again for any man that wild compulsion. The kind, when it had got out of control, that had led her down paths she never wanted to revisit.

Not now. Not ever.

She let the smile freeze on her face, stepped back and watched the other girl usher the handsome stranger to his table. She would hold off on her obligatory meet and greet to a new customer until she'd got herself together enough to mask her awareness of his appeal with breezy nonchalance. To use the light, semi-flirtatious tone that worked so well in hospitality.

Because, after all, he was just a stranger who'd breezed into town. She'd overreacted, big-time. She didn't need to fear that rush of attraction for an unsuitable man. He was just a customer she would never see again after he'd finished his lunch and moved on. He didn't even seem the kind of guy who would leave a generous tip.

Sam Lancaster knew he should be admiring the glorious view of the Dolphin Bay Harbour with its heritage-listed stone breakwaters, its fleet of fishing vessels and, beyond, the aquamarine waters of the Pacific Ocean. This stretch of the New South Wales south coast was known for its scenic beauty.

But he couldn't keep his eyes off the even more appealing view of the sassy, red-haired front-of-house manager who flitted from table to table in the Hotel Harbourside restaurant, pausing to chat with each customer about their orders.

Sam wasn't in the habit of flirting with strangers. He wasn't the type of man who always had a ready quip for a pretty flight attendant, a cute girl behind a bar or a hot new trainer at the gym. Consequently, he was stymied by his out-of-the-blue attraction to this woman.

She hadn't reached his table yet, and he found himself willing her to turn his way. In his head, he played over and over what clever remark he might utter when she did.

She wasn't movie-star beautiful, but there was a vibrancy about her that kept his gaze returning to her again and again: the way the sunlight streaming through the windows turned the auburn of her tied-back hair to a glorious, flaming halo. The sensual sway of her hips in the modest black skirt. The murmur of her laughter as she chatted to a customer. All were compelling. But, when she finally headed his way, the warmth of her wide smile and the welcome that lit her green eyes made him forget every word he had rehearsed.

Her smile was of the practised meet-and-greet type she'd bestowed on every other customer in the room. He knew that. But that didn't make it any less entrancing. She paused in front of his table. This close, he could see she had a sprinkling of freckles across the bridge of her nose and that her smile was punctuated with the most charming dimples.

What was a woman as sensational as this one doing in a backwater like Dolphin Bay?

Good manners prompted him get up to greet her, stumbling a little around the compact, ultra-modern chair not designed for a man of his height and build. Her startled step backwards made him realise she was just doing her job and a customer would usually remain seated. He gritted his teeth; he really wasn't good at this. Where was a clever quip when he needed one?

But she quickly recovered herself. 'Hi, I'm Kate Parker; welcome to Hotel Harbourside. Thank you for joining us for lunch.' Her voice was low and throaty without being self-consciously sexy and transformed the standard customer greeting spiel into something he'd like to put on a repeat loop.

He thrust out his hand in greeting. 'Sam Lancaster.'

Again she looked startled. He'd startled himself—since when did he shake hands with waitresses? But she took his hand in a firm, businesslike grip. He noted she wasn't wearing a ring of any kind.

'Hi, Sam Lancaster,' she said, her teasing tone making a caress of the everyday syllables of his name. 'Is everything okay at your table?'

He cleared his throat. 'F…fine.'

That was all he managed to choke out. Not one other word of that carefully thought out repartee.

Damn it.

He was a man used to managing a large, successful company. To never being short of female company if he didn't want it. But he couldn't seem to get it together in front of this girl.

He realised he'd gripped her warm, slender hand for a moment too long and he released it.

She glanced down at the menu on the table, then back up at him, the smile still dancing in her eyes. She knew. Of course she knew. A woman like this would be used to the most powerful of men stuttering in her presence. 'Have you ordered lunch yet? I can recommend the grilled snapper, freshly caught this morning.'

'Thank you, no. I'll order when my friend gets to the table.'

One winged auburn eyebrow quirked. 'Oh,' she said. 'A lady friend?' She flushed. 'Forgive me. None of my business, of course.'

'Nothing to forgive,' he said, pleased he'd given her cause to wonder about the sex of his lunch companion. 'While I'm waiting for *him,* I'm admiring the view of the harbour,' he said. 'It's really something.'

But the view of her was so much more enticing.

'No charge for the view,' she said. 'It's on the house.' She laughed, a low, husky laugh that made him think of slow, sensual kisses on lazy summer afternoons.

He couldn't look at her in case he gave away the direction of his thoughts. Instead he glanced to the full-length windows that faced east. 'I reckon it must be one of the most beautiful harbours on the south coast.'

'Hey, just on the south coast? I say the most beautiful in the whole of Australia,' she said with mock indignation.

'Okay. So it's the very best harbour in Australia—if not the world,' he agreed, playing along with her.

'That's better,' she said with a dimpled smile.

'I like the dolphins too.'

'You mean the real ones or the fake ones plastered on every building in town?'

'I didn't see them on *every* building,' he said. 'But I thought the dolphin rubbish bins everywhere had character.'

She put her hand on her forehead in a theatrical gesture of mock despair. 'Oh, please don't talk to me about those dolphin bins. People around here get into fights over whether they should go or they should stay, now Dolphin Bay has expanded so much. It was such a sleepy town when they were originally put up.'

'What do you think?' he asked.

'Me? I have to confess to being a total dolphin-bin freak. I love 'em! I adored them when I was a kid and would defend them to the last dorsal fin if anyone tried to touch them.'

She mimicked standing with her arms outstretched behind her as if there was something she was shielding from harm. The pretend-fierce look on her face was somewhat negated by her dimples.

In turn, Sam assumed a mock stance of defence. 'I'm afraid. Very afraid. I won't hurt your dolphin bins.'

Her peal of laughter rang out over the hum of conversation and clatter of cutlery. 'Don't be afraid.' She pretend-pouted. 'I'm harmless, I assure you.'

Harmless? She was far from harmless when it came to this instant assault on his senses.

'Lucky I said I liked the bins, then,' he said.

'Indeed. I might not have been responsible for my actions if you'd derided them.'

He laughed. She was enchanting.

'Seriously, though,' she continued. 'I've lived here for most of my life and I never tire of it, dolphins and all. April is one of the best times to enjoy this area. The water's still warm and the Easter crowds have gone home. Are you passing through?'

He shook his head. 'I'm staying in Dolphin Bay for the next week. I'll check in to the hotel after lunch.'

'That's great to hear.' She hit him with that smile again. 'I'm the deputy manager. It'll be wonderful to have you as our guest.'

Could he read something into that? Did she feel even

just a hint of the instant attraction he felt for her? Or was she just being officially enthusiastic?

'Let me know if there's anything you need,' she said.

A dinner date with you?

Gorgeous Kate Parker had probably spent longer than she should at his table. There were other customers for her to meet and greet. But Sam couldn't think of an excuse to keep her there any longer. He was going to have to bite the bullet and ask her out. For a drink; for dinner; any opportunity to get to know her.

'Kate, I—'

He was just about to suggest a date when his mobile phone buzzed to notify him of a text message. He ignored it. It buzzed again.

'Go on, please check it,' Kate said, taking a step back from his table. 'It might be important.'

Sam gritted his teeth. At this moment nothing—even a message from the multi-national company that was bidding for a takeover of Lancaster & Son Construction— was more important than ensuring he saw this girl again. He pulled the phone from his pocket and scanned the text.

He looked up at Kate. 'My friend Jesse is running late,' he grumbled. 'I hope he gets here soon. After a four-hour trip from Sydney, I'm starving.'

Kate's green eyes widened. 'Jesse?' Her voice sounded strangled. 'You mean...Jesse Morgan?'

'Do you know him? I guess you do.'

She nodded. 'Yes. It's a small town. I...I know him well.'

So Kate was a friend of Jesse's? That made getting to know her so much easier. Suddenly she wasn't just staff at the hotel and he a guest; they were connected through a mutual friend.

It was the best piece of news he'd had all day.

* * *

Kate was reeling. Hotter-than-hot Sam Lancaster was a friend of Jesse's? That couldn't, couldn't be. What unfair quirk of coincidence was this?

Despite her initial misgiving about Sam, she'd found she liked his smile, his easy repartee. She'd found herself looking forward to seeing him around the hotel. No way was she looking for romance—not with the Jesse humiliation so fresh. But she could admire how good-looking Sam was, even let herself flirt ever so lightly, knowing he'd be gone in a week. But the fact he was Jesse's friend complicated things.

What if Jesse had told Sam about the kiss disaster? She'd thought she'd fulfilled her cringe quotient for the day. But, at the thought of Sam hearing about the kiss calamity, she cringed a little more.

She should quickly back away from Sam's table. The last thing she wanted was to encounter Jesse not only in front of this gorgeous guy, but also the restaurant packed with too-interested observers, their gossip antennae finely tuned.

But she simply could not resist a few more moments in Sam Lancaster's company before she beat a retreat—maybe to the kitchen, at least to the other side of the room—so she could avoid a confrontation with Jesse when he eventually arrived.

'Where do you know Jesse from?' she asked, trying to sound chirpy rather than churning with anxiety.

'Jesse's a mate of mine from university days in Sydney,' Sam said in his deep, resonant voice. 'We were both studying engineering. Jesse was two years behind me, but we played on the same uni football team. We used to go skiing together, too.'

So that made Sam around aged thirty to her twenty-eight.

'And you've stayed friends ever since?' she said.

She'd so much prefer it if he and Jesse were casual acquaintances.

'We lost touch for a while but met up again two years ago on a building site in India, rebuilding the villages damaged in those devastating floods.'

She hadn't put darkly handsome Sam down as the type who would do active charity work in a far-flung part of the world. It was a surprise of the best kind.

'So you work for the same international aid organisation as Jesse?' she asked.

'No. I worked as a volunteer during my vacation. We volunteers provided the grunt work. In my case, as a carpenter.'

That figured. His hand had felt callused when she'd shaken it earlier.

'I'm seriously impressed. That's so…noble.' This hot, hunky man, who would have female hearts fluttering wherever he went, spent his hard-earned vacation working without pay in a developing country in what no doubt were dirty and dangerous conditions.

'Noble? That's a very nice thing to say, but I'd hardly call it that. It was hot and sweaty and damn hard work,' he said. 'I was just glad to be of help in what was a desperate situation for so many people.'

'I bet it wasn't much fun, but you were actually helping people in trouble. In my book, that's noble—and you won't make me think otherwise.'

He shrugged those impressively broad shoulders. 'It was an eye-opener. Sure made me appreciate the life I have at home.'

'I've thought about volunteering, but I've never actually done it. What made you sign up?'

His face tightened and shutters seemed to come down over his deep, brown eyes. 'It just seemed a good thing to do. A way to give back.' The tone of his voice made her wonder if he was telling her everything. But then, why should he?

Sam Lancaster was a guest—his personal life was none of her concern. In fact, she had to be careful not to overstep the mark of what was expected of a deputy manager on front-of-house duty on a busy Sunday.

It was as well to be brought back to reality.

She returned her voice to hospitality impartial. 'I'm so glad it worked out for you.' She glanced down at his menu. 'Do you want to order while you're waiting for Jesse?' It was an effort to say Jesse's name with such disinterest.

'I'll wait for him. Though I'm looking forward to exploring the menu; it looks very good.' Sam glanced around him and nodded approvingly. 'I like the way Ben built this hotel. No wonder it won architectural awards.'

'Ben, as in Jesse's brother? My boss? Owner of Hotel Harbourside?' She couldn't keep the incredulity from her voice.

'I'm friends with Ben as well as Jesse,' he said.

'Of course you would be,' she replied.

If she'd entertained for one moment the idea of following up her attraction to Sam Lancaster, she squashed it right now. She'd grown up with Ben too. The Morgans had been like family. The thought of conducting any kind of relationship with Sam under the watchful, teasing eyes of the Morgan brothers was inconceivable—especially if Jesse had told him about the kiss.

'Do you go way back with Ben, too?'

'He joined Jesse and me on a couple of ski trips to Thredbo,' said Sam. 'We all skied together.'

'More partying and drinking than actual skiing, I'll bet,' she said.

'What happens on ski trip, stays on ski trip,' said Sam with that devastating smile.

Individually, his irregular features didn't make for handsome. But together: the olive skin; the eyes as dark as bitter chocolate; the crooked nose; his sensual mouth; the dark, thick eyebrows, intersected by that intriguing small scar, added up to a face that went a degree more than handsome.

Jesse or Ben had not been hit with the ugly stick, either. She could only imagine what that trio of good-looking guys would have got up to in the party atmosphere of the New South Wales ski slopes. She knew only too well how wild it could be.

She'd gone skiing with her university ski-club during her third year in Sydney for her business degree. The snowfields were only a day's drive away from Sydney, but they might as well have been a world away.

Social life had outweighed skiing. That winter break they'd all gone crazy with the freedom from study, from families, from rules. If she'd met Sam then she would have gone for him, that was for sure. Instead she'd met someone else. Someone who in subsequent months had hurt her so badly she'd slipped right back into that teenage dream of kind, trustworthy Jesse. Someone who had bred the unease she felt at the thought of dating men with untamed good looks like Sam.

'So you're friends with Ben, too; I didn't know. We all went our separate ways during the time you guys must have met each other.' A thought struck her. 'Ah, now I get it. You're in Dolphin Bay for Ben and Sandy's wedding on Saturday.'

'Correct,' he said. 'Though I'm not one for weddings and all the waste-of-time fuss that surrounds them.'

Kate drew herself up to her full five-foot-five and put her hands on her hips in mock rebuke. 'Waste-of-time fuss? I don't know if I can forgive you for that comment as I happen to be the wedding planner for these particular nuptials.'

'Deputy manager of a hotel like this *and* a wedding planner? You're the very definition of a multi-tasker.'

'I'll take that as a compliment, thank you,' she said. 'I like to keep busy. And I like to know what's going on. Jesse calls me the self-appointed arbiter of everyone's business in Dolphin Bay.'

She regretted the words as soon as they'd slipped out of her mouth. Why, why, why did she have to bring up Jesse's name?

But Sam just laughed. 'That sounds like something Jesse would say. You must be good friends for him to get away with it.'

'We are good friends,' she said.

And that was all they ever should have been. When they'd been still just kids, they'd shared their clumsy, first-ever kiss. But it hadn't happened again until three days ago when she'd provocatively asked her old friend why it had been so long between kisses. A suggestion that had backfired so badly.

'What Jesse says is true,' she continued. 'He calls me a nosy parker. I like to call it a healthy curiosity about what's going on.'

'Necessary qualities for all your various occupations, I would think,' he said.

'Thank you. I think so too. I particularly need to be

on top of the details of Ben's wedding which is aaargh…'
she mimed tearing her hair out '…only six days away.'
She mentally ran through the guest list. 'Now I think of
it, there *is* a Sam on the guest list; I've been meaning to
ask Ben who it was. I don't know anything about him—
uh, I mean *you.*'

Sam spread out both hands in a gesture of invitation.
'I'm an open book. Fire away with the questions.'

She wagged a finger in mock-warning. 'I wouldn't say
that to a stickybeak like me. Give me carte blanche and
you might be here all day answering questions.' *What was
she saying?* 'Uh, I mean as they relate to you as a wedding guest, that is.'

'So I'll limit them,' he said. 'Five questions should be
all you need.'

*Five questions? She'd like to know a heck of a lot more
about Sam Lancaster than she could discover with five
questions.*

'Don't mind if I do,' she said.

Do you have a girlfriend, fiancée, wife?

But she ignored the first question she really wanted to
ask and chose the safe option. 'Okay, so my first question is wedding-menu related—meat, fish or vegetarian?'

'All of the above,' he said without hesitation.

'Good. That makes it easy. Question number two: what
do you plan to do in the days before the wedding? Do you
need me to organise any tours or activities?'

With me as the tour guide, perhaps.

He shook his head. 'No need. There's a work problem
I have to think through.'

She itched with curiosity about what that problem could
be—but questioning him about it went beyond the remit
of wedding-related questions.

'Okay. Just let me know if you change your mind.

There's dolphin-and whale-watching tours. Or hikes to Pigeon Mountain for spectacular views. Now for question number three: do you…?'

Something made her look up and she immediately wished she hadn't. *Jesse.* Coming in late for his lunch. She swallowed a swear word. Why hadn't she made her getaway while she could?

Too distracted by handsome Sam Lancaster.

Now this first post-kiss encounter with Jesse would have to be played out in front of Sam.

Act normal. Act normal. Smile.

But her paralysed mouth wouldn't form into anything other than a tight line that barely curved upwards. Nor could she summon up so much as a breezy 'hi' for Jesse— the man she'd been friends with all her life, had been able to joke, banter and trade insults with like a brother.

Jesse pumped Sam's hand. 'Sorry, I got held up.'

'No worries,' said Sam, returning the handshake with equal vigour.

'Kate,' said Jesse with a friendly nod in her direction, though she didn't think she was imagining a trace of the same awkwardness in his eyes that she was feeling. 'So you've already met my mate Sam.'

'Yes,' was all she managed to choke out.

'I see you got the best table in the house,' Jesse said to Sam, indicating the view with a sweep of his hand.

'And the best deputy manager,' said Sam gruffly, nodding to Kate.

'Why, thank you,' she said. For Sam, her smile worked fine, a real smile, not her professional, hospitality smile.

Jesse cleared his throat in a way she'd never heard before. *So he was feeling the awkwardness, too.*

'Yes; Kate is, beyond a doubt, awesome,' he said.

Kate recognised the exaggerated casualness of his tone. Would Sam?

'We're just friends,' Kate blurted out. She shot a quick glance at Sam to see a bemused lift of his eyebrow.

'Of course we're just friends,' Jesse returned, too quickly. He stepped around the table to hug her, as he always did when they met. 'Kate and I go way back,' he explained to Sam.

Kate stiffened as Jesse came near. She doubted she could ever return to their old casual camaraderie. It wasn't that Jesse had done anything wrong when he'd kissed her. He just hadn't done anything for *her*. He was probably a very good kisser for someone else.

But things had changed and she didn't want his touch, even in the most casual way. She ducked to slide away.

Big, big mistake.

Sam frowned as he glanced from her to Jesse and back again. Kate could see his mental cogs whirring, putting two and two together and coming up with something other than the zero he should be seeing.

It alarmed her. Because she really wanted Sam Lancaster to know there was nothing between her and Jesse. That she was utterly and completely single.

'Why don't you join us for lunch?' Jesse asked, pulling out the third chair around the table.

No way did she want to make awkward small talk with Jesse. The thought of using her three remaining questions to find out all about Sam Lancaster was appealing—but only when there was just him and her in the conversation.

She pointed her foot, clad in a black court pump, in the direction of the table. 'Hear the ball and chain rattling? Ben would have a fit if I downed tools and fraternised with the guests.'

Did she imagine it, or did Sam's gaze linger on her leg?

She hastily drew it back. 'Shame,' he said. He sounded genuinely regretful.

Not only did she want to walk away as quickly as she could from this uncomfortable situation but she also had her responsibilities to consider. She'd spent way too much time already chatting with Sam. 'Guys, I have to get back to work. I'll send a waitress over straight away and tell the chef to fill your order, pronto. I'm sure you both must be hungry.'

In an ideal world, she'd turn and walk away right now—and not return to this end of the room until both men had gone—but before she went there was wedding business to be dealt with.

'Jesse, will I see you this evening at Ben and Sandy's house for the wedding-planning meeting? We need to run through your best-man duties.'

'Of course,' said Jesse. 'And Sam will be there too.'

'Sam?' Ben had never mentioned that the Sam on the guest list would be part of the wedding party.

Sam shrugged those impressively broad shoulders. 'I've got business with Ben. He asked me to come along tonight.'

She'd anticipated seeing Sam around the hotel, but not seeing him so soon and in a social situation. She couldn't help a shiver of excitement at the thought. At the same time, she was a little put out she hadn't been informed of the extra person. Didn't her friends realise a wedding planner needed to know these things? What other surprises might they spring on her at this late stage?

Ben hadn't mentioned employing a carpenter. Were they planning on getting Sam to construct a wooden wedding arch on the beach where the ceremony was to be held? She wished they'd told her. They were counting down six days to the wedding.

But she would find that out later. Right now she *had* to get back to work.

'I'll see you tonight, Kate,' said Sam.

Did she imagine the promise she heard in his voice?

CHAPTER TWO

Sᴀᴍ ᴅɪᴅɴ'ᴛ ᴡᴀɴᴛ to have anything to do with weddings: whip-wielding wedding planners; mothers-of-the-bride going crazy; brides-to-be in meltdown; over-the-top hysteria all round. It reminded him too much of the ill-fated plans for his own cancelled wedding. Though it had been more than two years since the whole drama, even the word 'wedding' still had the power to bring him out in a cold sweat.

If it hadn't meant a chance to see Kate again he would have backed right out of the meeting this evening.

Now he stood on the sand at the bottom of the steps that led down from the hotel to the harbour beach. Jesse's directions to Ben's house, where the meeting was to be held, had comprised a vague wave in the general direction to the right of the hotel. He couldn't see a house anywhere close and wasn't sure where to go.

'Sam! Wait for me!'

Sam turned at the sound of Kate's voice. She stood at the top of the steps, smiling down at him. For a moment all he could do was stare. If he'd thought Kate had looked gorgeous in her waitress garb, in a short, lavender dress that clung to her curves she looked sensational.

She clattered down the steps as fast as her strappy sandals would allow her, giving him a welcome flash of pale, slender legs. Her hair, set free from its constraints, flowed all wild and wavy around her face and to her shoulders, the fading light of the setting sun illuminating it to burnished copper. She clutched a large purple folder under her arm and had an outsized brown leather bag slung over her shoulder.

She was animated, vibrant, confident—everything that attracted him to her. So different from his reserved, unemotional ex-fiancée. Or his distant mother, who had made him wonder as he was growing up whether she had wanted a son at all. Whose main interest in him these days seemed to be in how well he managed the company for maximum dollars on her allowance.

Kate came to a halt next to him, her face flushed. This close, he couldn't help but notice the tantalising hint of cleavage exposed by the scoop neck of her dress.

'Are you headed to Ben's place?' she asked.

'If I knew exactly where it was, yes.'

'Easy,' she said with a wave to the right, as vague as Jesse's had been. 'It's just down there.'

'Easy for a local. All I see is a boathouse with a dock reaching out into the water.'

'That *is* the house. I mean, that's where Ben and his fiancée, Sandy, live.'

'A boathouse?'

'It's the poshest boathouse you've ever seen.' Her face stilled. 'It was the only thing left after the fire destroyed the guesthouse where the hotel stands now.'

'Yes. I knew Ben lost his first wife and child in the fire. What a tragedy.'

'Ben was a lost soul until Sandy came back to Dolphin Bay. She was his first love when they were teenagers. It was all terribly romantic.'

'And now they're getting married.'

Kate laughed. 'Yes. Just two months after they met up again. And they honestly thought they were going to get away with a simple wedding on the beach with a glass of champagne to follow.'

'That sounds a good idea to me,' he said, more whole-heartedly than he had intended.

She looked at him, her head tilted to one side, curiosity lighting her green eyes. 'Really? Maybe, if you don't have family and friends who want to help you celebrate a happy-ever-after ending. Dolphin Bay people are very tight-knit.'

He wondered what it would be like to live in a community where people cared about each other, unlike the anonymity of his own city life, the aridity of his family life. 'Hence you became the wedding planner?'

'Yes. I put my hand up for the job. Unofficially, of course. The simple ceremony on the beach is staying. But they can't avoid a big party at the hotel afterwards. I aim to take the stress out of it for them.'

'Good luck with that.' He couldn't avoid the cynical twist to his mouth.

'Good planning and good organisation, more likely than mere luck.'

'You mean not too many unexpected guests like me?' he said.

Her flush deepened. 'Of course not. I'm glad Ben has invited a friend from outside.'

'From *outside?*'

'I mean from elsewhere than Dolphin Bay. From Sydney. The big smoke.'

He smiled. She might see Sydney as 'the big smoke', but he'd travelled extensively and knew Sydney was very much a small player on the world stage, much as he liked living there.

'My business with Ben could be discussed at a different time,' he said. 'I honestly don't know why they want me along this evening.'

'Neither do I.' She immediately slapped her hand over her mouth and laughed her delightful, throaty laugh. 'Sorry. That's not what I meant. What I meant was they hadn't briefed me on the need for a carpenter.'

He frowned. 'Pass that by me again?'

'You said you were a carpenter. I thought they were asking you tonight to talk about carpentry work—maybe an arch—though I wished they'd told me that before. I don't know how we'd secure it in the sand, and I haven't ordered extra flowers or ribbons or—'

'Stop right there,' he said. 'I'm not a carpenter.'

'But you said you worked in India as a carpenter.'

'As a volunteer. Yes, I can do carpentry. In fact, I can turn my hand to most jobs on a building site. My dad had me working on-site since I was fourteen. But my hard-hat days are behind me. I manage a construction company.'

He couldn't really spare the week away from the business in this sleepy, seaside town. But with the mega-dollar takeover offer for the company brewing, he needed headspace free of everyday demands to think.

The idea of selling Lancaster & Son Construction had first formed in India, where he'd escaped to after his cancelled wedding. In a place so different from his familiar world, he'd begun to think of a different way of life—a life he would choose for himself, not have chosen for him.

'So I'm not in the business of whipping up wedding arches,' he continued.

'Oh,' Kate said, frowning. 'I got that wrong, didn't I?' He already had the impression she might not enjoy being found mistaken in anything.

He threw up his hands in surrender. 'But, if they want a wedding arch, I'll do my best to build them one.'

'No, that's not it. That was only something I thought about. I wonder why they wanted you there, then?'

He smiled to himself at her frown. It was cute the way she liked to be in the know about everything.

'I've got business with Ben,' he said. 'I'm not sure if it's hush-hush or not, so I won't say what it is.'

She glanced down at her watch. 'Well, let's get there and find out, shall we?'

Kate started to stride out beside him in the direction of the boathouse. He noticed her feet turned out slightly as she walked. The financial controller at his company had a similar gait and she'd told him it was because she'd done ballet as a kid. Kate moved so gracefully he wondered if she was a dancer too. He'd like to see her moving her body in time to music—some sensual, driving rhythm. He could join her and…

Kate paused. 'Hang on for a minute. The darn strap on the back of these sandals keeps slipping down.'

She leaned down to tug the slender strap back into place, hopping on the other foot to keep her steady. She wobbled, lost her balance, and held on to his shoulder to steady herself with a breathless, 'Sorry.'

Sam wasn't sorry at all. He liked her close—her face so near to his, her warmth, her scent that reminded him of oranges and cinnamon. For a moment they stood absolutely still and her eyes widened as they gazed into each other's faces. He noticed what a pretty mouth she had, the top lip a classic bow shiny with gloss.

He wanted to kiss her.

He fisted his hands by his sides to stop him from reaching for her and pressing his mouth to hers.

He fought the impulse with everything he had.

Because it was too soon.

And he wasn't sure what the situation was between

Kate and Jesse. Earlier today, he hadn't failed to notice the tension between two people who had professed too vehemently that they were just friends.

Kate started to wobble again. Darn sandals; she needed to get that strap shortened. Sam reached out to steady her. She gasped at the feel of his hand on her waist, his warmth burning through the fine knit fabric of her dress. She wanted to edge away but if she did there was a very good chance she'd topple over into a humiliating heap on the sand.

She didn't trust herself to touch him or to be touched. Before she'd called out from the top of the steps, she'd paused to admire him as he'd stood looking out past the waters of Dolphin Bay to the open sea, dusk rapidly approaching. She'd been seared again with that overwhelming attraction.

But that was crazy.

She'd only just faced the reality that Jesse was not the man for her. That she'd been guilty—for whatever reason—of nurturing a crush for way too long on a man whom she only loved like a brother.

Of course, there had been boyfriends in the time between the two kisses. Some she remembered fondly, one with deep regret. But, in recent years, the conviction had been ticking away that one day Jesse and she would be a couple.

That kiss had proved once and for all that Jesse would never, ever be the man for her. There was no chemistry between them.

Could she be interested, so soon, in Sam Lancaster?

He'd changed to loose, drawstring cotton pants in a sludgy khaki and a collarless loose-weave white shirt—both from India, she guessed. The casual clothes made no secret of the powerful shape of his legs and behind, the well-honed muscles of his chest and arms—built up, she suspected, from his life as a builder rather than from hours in the gym.

Now, as he helped her keep her balance, she was intensely aware of the closeness of their bodies: his hand on her waist; her hand on his shoulder; the soft curve of her breast resting lightly against the hard strength of his chest. The hammering of her own heart.

Somewhere there was the swish of the small waves of the bay rushing onto the sand then retreating back into the sea; the rustle of the evening breeze in the trees that grew in the hotel garden; muted laughter from the direction of the boathouse.

But her senses were too overwhelmed by her awareness of Sam to take any of it in. She breathed in the heady aromas of masculine soap and shampoo that told her he was fresh out of the shower.

She was enjoying being close to him—and she shouldn't be. Three days ago, she'd wanted to kiss Jesse. How could she feel this way about a stranger?

She couldn't trust feelings that had erupted so easily. She needed time to get over the Jesse thing, to plan where she went to next. Not straight into another impossible crush, that was for sure.

Having Sam around was a distraction. He didn't look like the man who had battered her young heart—and a good portion of her soul—eight years ago when she'd been twenty, but he was the same type. Sam had that outrageous masculinity; the untamed, 'don't give a damn' look that sang to something wild and feminine and reckless in her—a part of herself she thought she'd long suppressed.

Panic started its heart-stopping, breath-stealing, muscle-tensing attack on her. She took in a deep breath that came out halfway to a sob.

'You okay?' Sam's deep voice was warm with concern.

She pretended to cough. 'F-fine thanks,' she said. 'Just…just a tickle in my throat.'

She dropped her hand from his shoulder and stepped away so his hand fell from her waist. She immediately felt bereft of his touch. With hands that weren't quite steady, she switched her handbag to her other shoulder.

'Let me carry that bag for you,' Sam said, taking it from her, his fingers grazing the bare skin of her arm. It was just a momentary touch but she knew she'd feel it for hours.

'Th-thanks,' she stuttered.

He heaved the bag effortlessly over his own shoulder. 'It weighs a ton; what on earth do you have in it?'

'Anything and everything. I like to be prepared in case anyone needs stuff. You know—tissues, insect repellent, pain-relievers, tamp— Never mind. My bag's a bit of a joke with my friends. They reckon anything they need they'll find in there.'

'And they probably rely on it. I get the impression you like to look after people.'

'I guess I do,' she said. There was no need to mention the accident that had left her sister in a wheelchair when Kate had been aged thirteen, or how her father had left and Kate had had to help out at home more than anyone else her age. How helping other people run their lives had become a habit.

'So what's in the folder?' he asked.

'The master plan for the wedding. The documents are on my tablet too, and my PC, but I've got backup printouts just in case. There's a checklist, a time plan, everyone's duties spelled out to the minute. I want this wedding to run like clockwork. I've printed out a running sheet for you too, to keep you up to speed, as they've made you part of the meeting.'

Schedules. Plans. Timetables. Keep the everyday aspects of life under control, and she'd have a better chance of keeping errant emotions and unwelcome longings under control.

She couldn't let Sam Lancaster disrupt that.

Sam noticed that as Kate spoke her voice got quicker and quicker. She was nervous. *Of him?*

Had she somehow sensed the tight grip he'd had to keep on himself to stop from pulling her into his arms?

He hadn't been looking for a relationship—especially not when everything was up in the air with the business. Selling it would impact not only on his life but also on the lives of the people employed by his company, including the contractors, suppliers and clients. It was important to weigh up the desire to free himself from the hungry corporate identity that had dominated his life since he'd been a child with the obligations due to those loyal to the company. He owed it to the memory of his father to get such a momentous decision right.

But in just the few short hours he'd been in Dolphin Bay Kate Parker had wiggled her lovely, vivacious way under his skin. He hadn't been able to think of anything else but seeing her again since he'd said goodbye to her at the restaurant.

And now he wanted to take her hand and walk her right past that boathouse—past the meeting she'd scheduled for a big wedding the bride and groom didn't seem to want and onto the beach with him, where she could ask him any questions she wanted and he could ask her a few of his own.

But he would not do that while there was any chance she could be involved with his good friend.

Again, she glanced down at the watch on her narrow wrist. 'C'mon, I can't bear to be late for anything—and especially for a meeting I arranged.'

He liked the dusting of freckles on her pale arms, so different from the orange-toned fake tan that was the standard for so many Sydney girls. He liked that she was so natural and unaffected, unlike the girls his mother, Vivien—she'd never liked him calling her Mum—kept trying to foist on him ever since the big society wedding she'd wanted for him had been called off.

'Let's go, then,' he said, trying to inject a note of enthusiasm into his voice. When they started talking flowers, caterers and canapés, he'd tune out.

Dusk was falling rapidly, as it did in this part of the world. The boathouse ahead was already in shadow, the lights from the windows casting a welcoming glow on the sand. There was music and the light hum of chatter. He thought he recognised Ben's laugh.

As Kate walked beside him, he realised she was keeping a distance away from him so that their hands would not accidentally brush, their shoulders nudge. He didn't know whether to be offended by her reaction to his closeness or pleased that it might indicate she was aware of the physical tension between them.

It was torture not knowing where he stood with her.

As they got within striking distance of the boathouse, he couldn't endure not knowing any longer. He wanted to put out his hand and stop her but he didn't trust himself to touch her again. He halted. She took a few more steps forward, realised he'd stopped and turned back to face him, a questioning look on her face.

Before she had time to speak, he did.

'Kate—stop. Before we go any further, I have to ask you something.'

'Sure,' she said, her head tilted to one side. 'Fire away. We've got a few minutes left before we're late.'

He prepared himself for an answer he didn't want to hear. 'Kate, what's the story with you and Jesse?'

CHAPTER THREE

KATE'S FACE FROZE in shock at his question. For a long moment she simply stared at him and Sam waited for her reply with increasing edginess.

'Me and J...Jesse?' she finally managed to stutter out.

Sam nodded. 'You said you were just friends. Is that true?'

'Yes. It is. Now.'

'What do you mean "now"?'

'You mean Jesse didn't say anything?'

'About you? Not a word.'

Kate looked down so her mass of wavy hair fell over her face, hiding it from him. She scuffed one sandal in the sand. Sam resisted the urge to reach out and push her hair into place. She did it herself, with fingers that trembled, and then looked back up at him. Even in the fading light he could see the indecision etched on her face. 'Do you want to hear the whole story? It's...it's kind of embarrassing.' Her husky voice was so low he had to dip his head to hear her.

Embarrassing? He nodded and tried to keep his face free of expression. He'd asked the question. He had to be prepared for whatever answer she might give him.

Kate clutched the purple folder tight to her chest. 'Our mothers were very close and Jesse, Ben and I grew up together. The mums were always making jokes about Jesse and me getting married in the future. You should see the photos they posed of us as little babies, holding hands.'

Sam could imagine how cute those photos would be, but he felt uncomfortable at the thought of that kind of connection being established between Kate and Jesse at such a young age. He had a vague recollection of Jesse once mentioning a red-haired girl back home. What had he said? Something about an ongoing joke in the family that if he and the girl never found anyone else they could marry each other…

Sam had found it amusing at the time. He didn't find it amusing right now. How difficult would it be to break such a long-standing bond?

'So that's the embarrassing bit?' he asked.

Kate pulled a face. 'It gets worse. When I was thirteen and he was fourteen we tried out our first ever kiss together. It was awkward and I ended up giggling so much it didn't go far. But I guess in my childish heart that marked Jesse as someone special.'

Jealousy seared through Sam at the thought of Jesse kissing Kate, even if they had been only kids. He was aware it was irrational—after all he hardly knew Kate—but it was there. It was real.

He had to clear his throat to speak. 'So you dated?'

She shook her head so vehemently her hair swung over her face. 'Never. We both dated other people. As teenagers, we cried on each other's shoulders when things went wrong. As adults, we lived our own lives. Until…'

Her brow creased as though she were puzzling out loud. 'Until a few years ago—I don't know why—I started to think Jesse might be the one for me. After all, everyone else thought so. I developed quite a crush on him.'

'So what's so embarrassing about that?'

She paused. 'Three days ago we kissed—at my suggestion.'

Now that jealousy turned into something that seethed in his gut. He'd always prided himself on being laid-back, slow to anger. He felt anything but laid-back at the thought of her in another man's arms, even one of his friends. Especially one of his friends.

'And?' His hands were fisted.

'Crush completely over. It was an utter disaster. So wrong that words can't describe it. And I speak for him as well as for me.'

Sam's fists slowly uncurled.

'So Jesse doesn't want you as more than a friend?'

'Heavens, no!' Her voice had an undertone of almost hysterical relief. 'We could hardly wait to make our getaways. And we succeeded in avoiding each other until we met in the restaurant earlier today.'

'It seemed awkward between you. Tense.'

'At first. But it's okay now. We've been friends for so long, seems we can both laugh it off as a monumental mistake and move on.'

With no more kissing, if Sam had anything to do with it.

He stepped closer to her. This time he did reach out and smooth an auburn curl from falling over her cheek. She started but didn't step away and he tucked it behind her ear before letting his hand drop back to his side. They stood as close as they could without actually touching.

'So Jesse's right out of the picture,' he said. 'Is there anyone else?'

Anyone else he had to fight for her?

Her face was half in shadow, half in the dim light coming from the boathouse. 'No one,' she said. 'I...I haven't dated for quite some time.' She paused. 'What about you? Question number three: is there any special lady in your life?'

'I was engaged to a long-term girlfriend. But no one special since that ended.'

He'd smarted for months at the way the engagement had been terminated, the wedding cancelled. In fact, he'd been so gutted he'd taken off to India to get away from the fallout. With perspective, he could see ending the engagement had been the right decision. But, while the wounds had healed, he had been wary of getting involved with anyone. Now he was ready. His ex had moved on, but he hadn't met a woman who had interested him. Until now.

'Oh,' she said. 'Would it count as question number four if I asked about what happened—or would that be part of question number three?'

He grinned. 'I'll allow it as part two of question three—but it might have to wait until I have more time to answer it.'

'I'm okay with that,' she said with a return of her dimples.

The last thing he wanted to do was scare Kate off. He had never before experienced this instant attraction to a woman. He had to work through how he handled it.

Kate was so obviously not the kind of woman for a no-strings fling. It wasn't what he wanted either. But his previous relationships had started off slowly with attraction growing. He understood how that worked, not this immediate flaming that might just burn itself out in a matter of days. The kind of flaming that had seen his parents trapped in an unhappy marriage, the consequences of which he had been forced to endure.

That aside, he realised Kate might not feel the same way as he did. If he wanted to get to know her, he knew he had to take things carefully.

'Before Jesse came into the restaurant, I was about to ask you out on a date,' he said. 'What would you have said?'

'I...I... You've taken me by surprise. I would have said—'

Just then the door of the boathouse opened, flooding them with further light. Ben peered through the door and called out. 'Hey, Kate, what are you doing out there? You warned us all to be on time or suffer dire consequences and now *you're* running late.'

Kate immediately stepped back from Sam so fast she nearly tripped. 'I'm coming!' she called in Ben's direction.

Sam cursed under his breath at the interruption. He wanted to shout at Ben to get lost.

Kate looked back up at Sam. 'Sam, I...'

But Ben was now heading towards them. He caught sight of Sam. 'Sam. Mate. I didn't see you there. Come on in.'

Sam groaned. Kate looked up at him in mute appeal. He shrugged wordlessly in a gesture of frustration. But not defeat; he would get Kate's reply sooner rather than later.

Then he was swept along into the boathouse with Kate, Ben walking between them like an old-fashioned chaperone.

An hour later, Kate was pleased at how well the meeting had gone. Everyone who needed to be there had been there—except for Sandy's sister who lived in Sydney, and her five-year-old daughter who was to be the flower girl. Plans had been finalised, timetables tweaked. Now the bridal party had been joined by a few other friends. Snack platters from the hotel kitchen had arrived and the barbecue was being fired up. There wasn't much more she could do to ensure the wedding went to plan on Saturday.

If only she hadn't been so darned conscious of Sam the entire time. It had been more than a tad distracting. She'd found herself struggling to remember important facts, her mind too occupied with Sam. But no one seemed to have noticed the lapse from her usual efficiency.

She just hoped they hadn't noticed the way she'd found herself compelled to check on him every few minutes. He'd met her glances with a smile, even a wink that had made her smother a laugh. It was only too obvious he was bored by the details of the wedding meeting. He'd crossed his long legs and uncrossed them. He'd not-so-subtly checked his mobile phone. He'd even nodded off for a few minutes until Ben had shoved him awake.

But she hadn't had a moment alone with him since they'd been interrupted on the beach.

She'd been just about to say yes to Sam's suggestion of a date. But would it really be a good idea?

Her fears screamed no. Just the light touch of his fingers on her cheek had practically sent her hurtling to the stars. She'd never felt such strong attraction so quickly. She was terrified that it might lead her into the kind of obsession that had nearly destroyed her in the past. It would be wisest to keep Sam at a distance.

But her loneliness urged yes to seeing Sam. Why shouldn't she go out with him on an uncomplicated, everyday date, with no other agenda than to share a meal, enjoy a movie, find out something about what made the other tick? Flirt a little. Laugh a lot. It didn't have to go further than that.

For so long she'd been on her own. Surely she deserved some masculine excitement in her life—even if only temporary? Sam would only be around for a week and then he'd be gone. Where was the harm in enjoying his company?

It was time to say yes to that date.

She'd lost sight of him—difficult in the space of the boathouse, which was basically just one large room converted into luxury living. He must have escaped outside to the barbecue. She'd go find him.

Before she could make the move, the bride-to-be, Sandy, sidled up beside her. 'Sooo,' she said in a teasing tone. 'You and that gorgeous hunk, Sam Lancaster...'

Kate couldn't help it; she flushed again and Sandy noticed. That was the problem with being a fair-skinned redhead: even the slightest blush flamed. 'What about me and Sam?' she said, knowing she sounded unnecessarily defensive.

'You've hardly kept your eyes off him all evening. And he you. I reckon he's smitten. And maybe you are too.'

'Of course he's not. Of course I'm not.'

'Oh, really?' said Sandy in an overly knowing tone.

Kate narrowed her eyes. 'Are you by any chance paying me back for the way I poked my nose in with you and Ben when you first came back to Dolphin Bay?'

Kate had been overprotective of her friend Ben when Sandy had showed up out of the blue after twelve years of no contact. But she'd very soon warmed to Sandy and they'd become good friends.

'Don't be silly,' said Sandy. 'I'm so deliriously happy with Ben, I want you to be happy too. Sam is really nice, as well as being a hunk. I got the lowdown on him.'

'I only met him today. Nothing is happening there, I can assure you.'

Nothing except her heart starting to race every time she caught a glimpse of him towering over the other guests.

'But it might. You know what they say about what happens at weddings.' Sandy smiled. 'The bridesmaid and the groomsman...'

Kate frowned. 'I don't know what you mean. I'm your

bridesmaid. But Sam isn't Ben's groomsman. I should know, as your wedding planner.'

'Uh, think again. Right now, Ben's asking Sam to be just that.'

'What? I thought he only wanted a best man?'

'He's changed his mind. My sister Lizzie, as chief bridesmaid, will be partnered by the best man, Jesse. That means you'd be coming up that beach aisle by yourself. We thought why not even things up by partnering you with Sam? You'll easily be able to readjust your ceremony schedules. That is, if Sam agrees to it.'

Kate tried to tell herself she was being oversensitive but she could sense that echo again: *poor Kate.*

'Sandy, it's so sweet of you, but is this about what happened with Jesse and me three days ago? If so, I—'

Sandy's hazel eyes were kind. 'Kate, I'm so sorry it didn't work out with Jesse. I know how much you've always wanted him.'

Kate swallowed hard. It was so difficult to talk about it. 'Did I really, though, Sandy? I think maybe I dreamed of a kind, handsome man—so different from the men I'd dated—and Jesse was there. I…I fixated on him. It wasn't real.'

'You could be right. To tell you the truth, I didn't ever see any chemistry between you.'

Kate giggled. 'There was no chemistry whatsoever. I can't tell you how much I regretted it. I couldn't run away fast enough.'

'I bet you wouldn't run too far if you were alone with Sam Lancaster. Doesn't he fit the bill? He's handsome, all right—and he must be kind, or he wouldn't have been off volunteering in India, would he?'

Kate sobered. 'All that. But, Sandy, don't try to match-make, will you? I don't want a pity party. I'm not desperate for a man.'

Sandy put her hand reassuringly on Kate's arm. 'Of course you're not. But is it a bad thing for your friends to look out for you? And for you to let them? You've got to admit, it's more fun being a bridesmaid if you have a handsome groomsman in tow.'

'Of course it is. And you're right; you don't get more handsome than Sam Lancaster. And he's interesting, too.' She found herself looking over her shoulder to watch out for him, only to see him coming back into the room with Ben. 'Here he is. I hope he didn't hear me twittering on about how handsome he is,' she whispered to Sandy.

She watched as Sam and Ben approached. Funny; she'd always found Ben so imposing, Jesse so good-looking. But Sam outshone any man she'd ever met in terms of pure, masculine appeal.

'So did Sam say yes to being groomsman, Ben?' asked Sandy.

'Of course he did,' said tall, blond Ben.

Sam stood shoulder-nudging distance from Kate. She could feel his warmth, smell the hint of bourbon on his breath. 'As if I had a choice, when I heard who would be the bridesmaid I was escorting,' he said with a smile that was just for her. She smiled back, glad beyond reason to have him by her side.

She would ask *him* on a date. ASAP.

Now the planning part of the evening was over and her duties done, she could get the heck out of there and take Sam with her, so they could talk in private away from too-interested eyes.

But Ben had other ideas. He turned to Kate. 'I was going to introduce you to Sam tonight, but as you've already met I'll cut straight to the chase.'

Kate sighed inwardly. All she could think of was being alone with Sam. But she was aware that, while Ben was a long-time friend, he was also her boss. He had his boss voice on now; she almost felt she should be taking notes.

'Yes, sir,' she said flippantly, at the same time wondering how a work thing could possibly involve Sam.

'We've finally got planning approval for the new resort,' said Ben with a whoop of triumph.

'Really?' she said, scarcely able to let herself believe the news. 'Really and truly?'

'Really,' said Ben with a huge grin.

'Congratulations, Kate,' said Sandy, hugging her. 'I know how hard you worked with Ben on the submission.'

Momentarily lost for words, Kate hugged Sandy back. Then she looked from Sam to Ben to Sam again. 'That's amazing. After all the hours we put in, I can hardly believe it's actually happening,' she said.

She grabbed hold of Sam's arms and did a little jig of excitement—then realised what she'd done and dropped her hands. She pulled a face. 'Sorry. I got carried away.'

'Don't be sorry,' he said. 'I can see this means a lot to you.'

Ben put up his hand. 'Wait. There's more. Sam's company is going to build the resort. Lancaster & Son Construction is one of the biggest and the best in the country. We're fortunate to have him on board.'

Kate stared, too astounded to say anything. *Why hadn't she known this?*

When she finally got her breath back, Kate turned to Sam. 'So that was the hush-hush business.'

And she'd thought he was a carpenter.

'Not so hush-hush now,' he said.

'I can't tell you how thrilled I am about this project,' she said. 'A luxury, boutique spa resort nestled in the bush on that beautiful spot. It's on land overlooking Big Ray Beach—that's our surf beach—with incredible views. The resort's a big deal for Dolphin Bay.'

'And a triumph for Kate. It was initially her idea,' Ben explained to Sam. 'As her reward for kick-starting it, she has equity.'

Her ownership was only measured in the tiniest of percentages—a token, really—but Kate intended to be a hands-on manager once the resort was up and running. It would be her dream job, something she wanted so much it hurt.

'Congratulations,' said Sam. 'It's great to hear you're such an entrepreneur.'

Kate basked in the admiration she saw in his eyes. At age twenty-eight, she'd had a few false starts to her career; now she was exactly where she wanted to be. 'I'm still a bit dazed that it's actually going to happen,' she said.

Ben turned to Kate. 'I want you to be our liaison person with Sam—starting from now. I'll be away on my honeymoon after next week and this week too caught up with work at the hotel.'

She blinked at Ben. 'Th..that's a surprise.'

'But it makes sense,' said Ben. 'You know more about the project than anyone else but me. You can start by taking Sam to the site for him to take a look at it. That okay with you, Sam?'

'Of course,' said Sam, though Kate thought he looked perturbed.

'I'll leave you to two to discuss the details,' said Ben, ushering Sandy away.

Finally Kate was left alone with Sam, exactly what she'd longed for all evening. She'd never been more aware of his big, broad-shouldered body, his unconventionally handsome face.

Only now she would value a few minutes on her own to think over what had just happened.

Ten minutes ago she'd been ready to drag him outside and arrange a date. Or two. Except now things were very different. She would have to put all such thoughts on hold. Sam was no longer a stranger blown into town for a week, never to be seen again. He was someone with ongoing links to Dolphin Bay. She'd be working with him as a professional in a business capacity.

How could she possibly think she could have any kind of personal relationship with him?

CHAPTER FOUR

SAM HAD BEEN knocked sideways by the news that he'd be working with Kate on Ben's new resort development. He'd always enforced a strict rule in the company—no dating clients. Without exception. Not for his employees, not for him. He'd amended a number of his father's long-standing edicts when he'd taken over but not that one. It made good business sense.

How ironic that it now applied to Kate—and company protocol was too important to him to have one rule for the boss and another for the rest of the team.

He felt like thumping the wall with his clenched fist, right through the tastefully restored wooden boards. He clenched his jaw and uttered a string of curse words under his breath.

He had to get out of this room. On top of his frustration, he felt stifled by all the wedding talk buzzing around him. When it came to his turn to get hitched—his own derailed wedding hadn't turned him off the idea of getting married one day—he thought elopement would be a great idea.

Then there were the overheard murmurs that had him gritting his teeth. They had all been along the lines of what a shame it was about Kate and Jesse—immediately hushed when he'd come near. Whether that was because they saw him as an interloper, or they could tell he was interested in Kate, he didn't know. But he didn't like it.

Everything he'd heard about the oppressive nature of small-town life was true.

He hated everyone knowing his business. How Kate could bear it was beyond his comprehension. Anything smaller than Sydney, with its population of more than four-and-a-half million, would never be for him.

A middle-aged woman was bearing down on them. No doubt she wanted Kate's opinion on the colour of ribbons on a flower arrangement or some such waste-of-space frivolity.

'I'm going outside for some air,' he muttered to Kate and strode away before the woman reached them.

He realised his departure was being watched with interest by everyone else in the room. Tough. There'd be nothing for them to gossip about now. Kate was strictly out of bounds.

It was dark outside now but the moon was full, reflecting on the quietly rippling waters of the bay. He gulped in the cool evening air, then let out those curse words at full volume as he kicked at the solid base of a palm tree as hard as he could.

His first thought was that after the site inspection tomorrow he would get the hell out of Dolphin Bay. But he'd promised to be Ben's groomsman. He cursed again. He was trapped here—with a woman he wanted but suddenly couldn't have.

The door opened behind him, a shaft of light falling on the deck. He moved away. He was in no mood to talk. To Ben. To Jesse. To anyone.

'Sam?' Her voice was tentative but even without turning around he knew it was Kate.

He turned. There was enough moonlight so he could

see the anxiety on her face. She was wringing her hands together. He ached to reach out to her but he kept his hands fisted by his sides.

'Let's walk out to the end of the dock,' she said. 'You feel like you're on a boat out there. And no one can over-hear us.'

He fell into step beside her. A row of low-voltage sensor lights switched on to light them to the dock. The builder in him admired the electrics. His male soul could only think of the beautiful woman beside him and regret about what might have been.

They reached the end of the dock without speaking. A light breeze coming off the water brought with it the tang of the sea and lifted and played with the soft curls around Kate's face. She seemed subdued, as if the moonlight had sucked all that wonderful vivacity from her.

She turned to him. 'I had no idea you were building the resort.'

'I had to keep it confidential. I didn't know you were involved in any way.'

'It was the first time I heard I was to liaise with you. I hadn't seen that coming.' She looked up at him. Her face was pale in the weak, shimmering light, her eyes shad-owed. 'This...this changes things, doesn't it?'

'I'm afraid it does,' he said, knowing from the regret in her eyes that she was closing the door on him before it got any more than halfway open.

'It...it means I have to say no to that date,' she said.

One part of him was plunged into dismay at the tolling finality of her words, the other was relieved that he hadn't had to say them first.

'It means I have to rescind the offer,' he said gruffly. 'I have an iron-clad no-dating-the-clients rule.'

Her short, mirthless laugh was totally unlike her usual

throaty chime. 'Me too. I've never thought it was a good idea. There can be too many consequences if the dating doesn't work out but you still have to work together.'

'Agreed,' he said. 'There are millions of dollars at stake here.' And his company's reputation—especially at the time of a publicly scrutinised buy-out bid. The company had to come first again—as it always did. This time, it came ahead of him dating the only woman who had seriously interested him since his broken engagement. Again he had that sense of the business as a millstone, weighing him down with protocol and obligation—as it had since he'd been fourteen years old.

Kate laughed that mirthless laugh again. 'Funny thing is, I suspect it's Ben's clumsy attempt at matchmaking and it's totally backfired.'

He gave a snort of disbelief. 'You think so?'

'The groomsman thing? The cooked-up excuse to get me to show you the land when there's no real need for me to?'

'My take on it is that Ben thought you knew more than anyone else about the plans for the new resort. You were the best person for the job. Why would you believe any differently?'

'I guess so,' she said with a self-deprecating quirk of her pretty mouth. 'But the out-of-the blue request to be a groomsman?'

Sam snapped his fingers. 'I get it—you were concerned an extra member of the wedding party would put your schedules out?'

Her smile was forced as she raised her hand. 'Guilty! I guess I *was* a little disconcerted about that. But I mainly felt bad for you being coerced into being a groomsman on such a trumped-up excuse. You don't seem to be comfortable with all the wedding stuff—I saw you yawning during the meeting. Then you get thrown in at the deep end.'

'Ben didn't have to coerce me to be his groomsman. I liked the idea of being your escort at the wedding.'

Wouldn't any red-blooded male jump at the chance to be with such a gorgeous girl? Or had Jesse done such a number on her she didn't realise how desirable she was?

Truth be told, if it hadn't been for the prospect of more time with Kate, he'd rather have stayed a guest and stood apart from the wedding tomfoolery. Now he would have to spend the entire time with Kate, knowing she was off-limits. It would be a kind of torture.

'Thank you,' she said. 'It will be nice to have you there. It might have been awkward with Jesse otherwise. People would have been gossiping. Even though...'

'It has to be strictly business between us now.'

'Yes,' she said. 'I...I realise that.'

The tinkling, chiming sound of rigging against masts from the boats moored in the harbour carried across the water, adding to the charm of the setting. Dolphin Bay was a nice part of the world, he conceded. For a visit, for work—a vacation, perhaps—but not to live here.

'We should be going back to the others,' she said with a notable lack of enthusiasm.

'Yes,' he said, without making a move.

The last place he wanted to be was back in the boat-house. He liked being out here on the dock talking to her, even if the parameters of the conversations they could have had now had been constrained.

Suddenly she slapped her hand on her arm. 'Darn mosquitoes!'

She reached into that capacious shoulder bag, burrowed around and pulled out a can. 'Insect repellent,' she explained.

'You really do have everything stashed in there,' he said, amused.

'Even a single mosquito buzzing its way down the coast will seek me out and feast on my fair skin.' As she spoke, she dramatised her words and mimed the insect dive-bombing her in a totally unself-conscious manner.

Lucky mosquito. Sam could imagine nuzzling into the pale skin of her throat—kissing, nibbling, even a gentle bite...

That was forbidden territory now.

'Want some?' she asked.

Mosquito spray? 'No thanks. They never bother me.'

'Lucky you.' She stood away from him and sprayed her legs and arms with a spray that smelled pleasantly of lavender.

'You're not suited to beach-side living, are you?' he asked when she came close again.

'Not really,' she said. 'Insects adore me and I burn to a frizzle if I'm out in the sun in the middle of the day. But I love to swim, and the mornings and evenings are great for that.'

A moonlight swim: her pale body undulating through the shimmering water, giving tantalising glimpses of her slender limbs, her just-right curves; he shrugging off his clothes and joining her...

This kind of scenario was not on. Not with a client.

He cleared his throat. 'I like to start the day with a swim. Where do you recommend?' he asked.

'The bay is best for quiet water. Then there's Big Ray surf beach—you get to it via the boardwalk. Around from there is an estuary where the freshwater river meets the sea. It's magic. Not many people go there and you can swim right up that river without seeing another soul. Oh, except for the occasional kangaroo coming down to drink.'

'It sounds idyllic,' he said.

'That's a good word for it. I can show you how to get there on the map. I'd offer to take you but that's—'

'Not a good idea,' he said at the same time she did. Not with him in his board shorts and her in a bikini. Or, with that fair skin of hers, did she wear a sleek, body-hugging swimsuit?

A cold sweat broke out on his forehead. Somehow he had to stop himself from thinking of Kate Parker as anything other than a client. She was the Hotel Harbourside client liaison. Nothing more.

'I'll have to have a word with Ben,' said Kate. 'About his matchmaking efforts, I mean—well-meaning but misguided.'

'Ben's an amateur. You haven't seen misguided matchmaking until you've met my mother. She's a master of it.'

Why had he said that?

Why not?

Kate was a client. That didn't mean he couldn't have a personal conversation with her.

'But not successfully?' Kate asked.

What had she called herself? A stickybeak. It was such an Aussie expression but so perfectly summed up a person who couldn't resist sticking their noses into other people's business. He preferred her description of herself as having a healthy curiosity. And right now he could tell it had been piqued.

'I veto all her efforts,' he said. 'I might work in the family firm but I run my own life.'

That hadn't always been the case. His father had been overly domineering. His mother had just wanted him kept out of her hair. There'd been an almighty battle when his mother had planned to send him to boarding school— with his father victorious, of course. As a child he'd had no choice but to go along with the way they'd steered his life. As a teenager he'd rebelled against his father but still had little choice. The real confrontation hadn't come until he'd turned twenty-one, nine years ago.

'Your mother—she's in Sydney?' Kate asked.

An image of his mother flashed before his eyes: whippet-thin in couture clothes, hair immaculate, perfectly applied make-up that could not disguise the lines of discontent around her mouth or the disappointment in her eyes when she looked at her son. Her son who'd chosen to follow his father into the rough and tumble of the construction industry—not a law degree or a specialist medical degree she saw as more socially acceptable. Not that she ever complained about the hefty allowance the company brought her.

He looked at Kate in the moonlight, at her hair, a glorious mass of riotous waves, her simple dress, her eyes warm with real interest in what he had to say. She seemed so straightforward. So genuine. Never had two women been more different.

'Yes. She'd never stray from the eastern suburbs.'

'And your father? I wondered about the "and son" bit in your company name. Are you the son?'

'You realise that's question number four?' he said.

'I guess it is,' she said. Her dimples had snuck back into her smile but now they disappeared again. 'Sorry. I guess I shouldn't ask more questions now...now things have changed.'

'As a business client? Why not? Fire away.'

'And, in fact, it's a three-part question.'

'Well, number two was a two-part question.'

'I start as I mean to continue.'

'So I've got a four-part question to look forward to in the next stage of my interrogation?'

'Maybe. I'll keep you guessing.' Her delightful laughter echoed around the beach. 'But in the meantime, do you want to answer part one of question four?'

'My father died three years ago.'

The laughter faded from her voice. 'I'm so sorry. Was it expected?'

'A sudden heart attack. He was sixty-seven and very fit.'

'How awful for you. And for your mother.'

'It was a shock for her. She was my father's second wife and considerably younger than he was. Didn't expect to be left on her own so soon.'

'And you?' Her voice was gentle and warm with concern. 'It must have been a terrible shock for you too.'

He'd been in Western Australia when he'd got the phone call, a six-hour flight away. He'd never forgiven himself for not being there. He'd been so concerned with proving himself to his father by fixing the problems in Western Australia, he had missed his chance to say goodbye to him.

'Yes. Worse in some ways, because suddenly I had to take over the running of the company. I hadn't expected to have to do that for years to come.'

'That was a truckload of responsibility.'

He shrugged. 'The old man had been preparing me for the role since I'd been playing with my Lego, teaching me the business from the ground up. He was a tough taskmaster. I didn't get any privileges for being the boss's son. I had to earn my management stripes on my own merits.'

'Still, actually taking the reins of such a large company must have been scary.'

'The first day I took my place at the head of the boardroom table was as intimidating as hell. All those older guys just waiting for me to make a mistake.' He had never admitted that to anyone. *Why Kate? Why now?*

'But you won their respect, I'll bet.'

'I worked hard for it.' Too hard, perhaps. He hadn't had time for much else, including his fiancée. That was when she had started accusing him of being an obsessive workaholic who put the company ahead of everything else—particularly her. He'd come to see some truth in her accusations.

'Good for you; that can't have been easy,' said Kate. 'Which brings me back to question four—you're the son in the company name?'

'Actually, the son was my father. My grandfather started the company, building houses in the new suburbs opening up after the Second World War. My dad grew the company far bigger than my grandfather could ever have dreamed. In turn, I've taken it even further.'

'Obviously you build hotels.'

'And office towers and shopping malls and stadiums. All over the country. Even outside the country.'

In the three years he'd been at the helm he'd steered the business through tough economic times. He had pushed it, grown it. He didn't try to hide his pride in his achievements. They'd come at a cost—his personal life.

Kate went quiet again. 'You must have thought I was an idiot for suggesting you were here to build a wedding arch.'

'Of course I didn't think you were an idiot. I'm a builder. I can make arches. Fix drains. Even turn my hand to electrical work if I have to.' He held out his hands. 'With the calluses to prove it.'

She turned away so she looked out to sea and he faced her profile—her small, neat nose, her firm, determined chin. 'But you're also the CEO of a huge construction company. That's quite a contradiction.'

And now she was his client.

He realised the distance their business roles now put between them. Once more his commitment to the company came over his personal happiness. It was a price he kept on paying.

And he wasn't sure he was prepared to do that any longer.

Kate found it difficult to suppress a sigh. *Be careful what you wish for.*

She hadn't wanted to be distracted by Sam while she sorted out her life after the Jesse issue. Now Sam could not be anything more than a business connection.

Her disappointment was so intense she felt nauseous, choked by a barrage of what might have beens. She hadn't been able to get him off her mind since he'd walked into the restaurant. But how did she stop herself from being attracted to him?

Because the more she found out about him, the more she liked him.

Still, she had had practice at putting on a mask, at not showing people what she really felt. At hiding her pain. At being cheerful, helpful, always-ready-to-help-out Kate.

She would simply slip into the impersonal role of client, hide her disappointment that she couldn't spend time with Sam in any other capacity. She must remember to thank Ben for the opportunity to deal with the CEO of the company building her dream hotel.

It was probably for the best, anyway. She wasn't ready for romance, especially with someone who lived so far away. The four hours to Sydney might as well be four hundred as far as she was concerned. One of the reasons Jesse had been appealing was that, although he worked overseas now, he intended to settle in Dolphin Bay.

She looked down at her watch, the dial luminous in the dark.

'We really should be getting back,' she said, aiming for

brisk and efficient but coming out with a lingering, 'don't really want to go just yet' tone that wouldn't fool anyone as smart as Sam.

'I like it out here,' he said. He hunkered down on the very end of the dock then swung his long legs over the edge. He patted the place next to him in invitation. 'No one will have missed us.'

Against her better judgement, she joined him. She was hyper-aware of his warmth, his strength, his masculinity, and she made sure she sat a client-like distance from him so their shoulders didn't touch. The water slapped against the supports of the pier and a fish leapt up out of the water, glinting silver in the moonlight, and flopped back in with a splash.

'You're right; it's like being on a boat,' Sam said.

'Without the rocking and the seasickness.'

'Or the feeling of being trapped and unable to get off exactly when you want to.'

Her eyes widened. 'You feel that way about boats too?'

'I've never much cared for them. Which is at odds with living on the harbour in Sydney.'

'Me neither,' she said. 'I'd rather keep my feet firmly planted on land.'

'*Definitely* not a seaside person.'

'In another life I'd probably live in a high-rise in the middle of the city and go to the ballet and theatre on the nights I wasn't trying the newest restaurants.' Now she did indulge in the sigh. 'Trouble is, I love it here so much. I wasn't joking earlier when I said I thought it was the most beautiful place in Australia.'

'That hasn't escaped my attention,' he said.

'It's familiar and s—' She hastily bit off the word 'safe' and said, 'So relaxed.'

'It's nice, I'll give you that. But have you been to many places to compare?' he asked.

'Do I really sound like a small-town hick?'

'Anything but,' he said. 'I was just interested. I've travelled a lot; we might have been to the same places.'

'Sure, I've been to lots of other places. When I…after I…'

She struggled to find the right words that wouldn't reveal the back story she had never shared with anyone: the reason she'd left university in Sydney without completing her degree. The reason she felt she would always doubt her choice of men. 'I toured all around the country in a small dance company.'

'I thought you might have been a dancer,' he said. She followed his gaze down to where her feet dangled over the edge of the pier.

'Let me guess—because of the duck walk? Years of training in classical ballet tends to do that. Only, we dancers call it "a good turn-out".'

'I was going to say because of the graceful way you move.'

'Oh,' she said and the word hung still in the air.

She blushed that darn betraying blush. She wasn't sure how to accept the compliment. Mere hours ago she might have replied with something flirtatious. But not now. Not when all that was off the agenda.

'Thank you,' was all she said.

'Would I have heard of your dance company?'

'I highly doubt it. It was a cabaret troupe and far from famous. We toured regional Australia—the big clubs, town halls, civic centres, small theatres if they had them. Once we had a stint in New Zealand. We were usually the support act to a singer or a magician—that kind of thing. It was hard work but a lot of fun.'

'Was?'

'A dancer's life is a short one,' she said, trying to sound unconcerned. 'I injured my ankle and that was the end of it.'

She didn't want to add that her ankle had healed—but the emotional wounds from a near-miss assault from a wouldn't-take-no-for-an-answer admirer had not.

During the time the man had had her trapped, he'd taunted her that her sexy dance moves in body-hugging costumes made men think she was asking for it. Coming so soon after her damaging relationship with her university boyfriend, she'd imploded. She hadn't performed since, or even danced at parties.

'I'd like to see you dance some day,' Sam said.

'Chance would be a fine thing. I don't dance at all any more.'

Sadness wrenched at her as it always did when she thought about dance. To express herself with movement had been an intrinsic part of her and she mourned its loss.

'Because of the ankle?' he said.

'Yes,' she lied.

She felt uncomfortable with the conversation focused on her. That was a time of her life she'd sooner forget. She made her voice sound bright and cheery. That was what people expected of her. 'You do realise you've skipped answering part two of question four,' she said.

'I did?'

'You know, about why your engagement ended?' she prompted. 'Unless that's off the agenda now for discussion between business associates.'

'No secrets there,' he said. 'Two weeks before the wedding my former fiancée, Frances, called it off. I hadn't seen it coming.'

'That must have been a shock. What on earth happened?'

Kate really wanted to hear his reply. She couldn't understand how anyone engaged to be married to Sam Lancaster could find any reason to call it off. She could scarcely believe it when—just as Sam was about to answer her—she heard her name being called from the boathouse.

She stilled. So did Sam. 'Pretend you don't hear it,' Sam muttered in an undertone.

She tried to block her ears but her name came again, echoing over the water. Sandy's voice.

'Over here,' she called, then mouthed a silent, 'Sorry,' to Sam.

Sandy rushed along the dock. 'Thank heaven you hadn't gone home. Lizzie, my sister, just phoned. She can't make it to the hen and stag night on Wednesday. We'll have to drive up to Sydney and have it there instead.'

'But I—'

'Don't worry, Kate,' said Sandy. 'I promise it won't be any more work for you.' Sandy turned to Sam. 'Are you okay with the change of plan?'

Sam shrugged. 'Sure.'

Kate cleared her throat against the rising panic that threatened to choke her. She couldn't go to Sydney. She just couldn't. But she didn't want to tell Sandy she wouldn't be going with them. She couldn't cope with the explanations, the reasons. She'd make her excuses at the last minute. They could party quite happily without her.

'Fine by me too,' she said, forcing a smile. 'One less thing for me to have to organise.'

CHAPTER FIVE

UP UNTIL NOW, Sam had never had a problem with the 'no dating the clients' rule. Along the way there had been attractive female clients who had made their personal interest in him clear. But he had had no trouble deflecting them; the business had always come first.

It was a different story with Kate Parker. Kate certainly wasn't coming on to him in any way. In fact, she couldn't be more professional. This morning she had picked him up from the hotel. On the short drive to the site of the proposed resort, the conversation had been completely business-related—not even a mention of the wedding, let alone their thwarted date.

He was the one who was having trouble seeing her purely as a client and not as a beautiful, desirable woman who interested him more than anyone had interested him for a long time. It was disconcerting the way she appeared so easily to have put behind her any thought of a more personal relationship.

The thought nagged at him—if Ben hadn't appointed her as his liaison would she have agreed to that date? Might they have been going out to dinner together tonight?

She was a client. Just a client.

But as she guided him around the site he found her presence so distracting it was a struggle to act professionally.

The way her hair gleamed copper in the mid-morning sun made even the most spectacular surroundings seem dull by comparison. When she walked ahead of him in white jeans, and a white shirt that showcased her shapely back view, how could he objectively assess the geo-technical aspects of the site? Or gauge the logistics of crane access when her orange cinnamon scent wafted towards him?

He gritted his teeth and kicked the sandy soil with its sparse cover of indigenous vegetation, filling his nostrils with the scent of eucalypt leaves crushed underfoot.

Truth be told, he didn't really need to inspect the site. The company had a team of surveyors and engineers to do that. He'd promised Ben he'd take a look more as a courtesy than anything. Now Kate was standing in for Ben and it was a very different experience than it would have been tramping over the land with his old skiing buddy.

'What do you think?' Kate asked.

She twirled around three-hundred-and-sixty degrees, her arms outstretched. Pride and excitement underscored her voice. She'd seemed subdued when he'd said goodnight at the boathouse—thrown by the last-minute change to the stag night. But there was no trace of that today. It appeared she could take change in her stride. He admired that—in his experience, not all super-organised people were as flexible.

'It's magnificent,' he said. *You're magnificent.* 'You're on to a winner.'

The large parcel of land stood elevated above the northern end of what the locals called Big Ray beach, though there was another name on the ordinance surveys. Groves of spotted gums, with their distinctive marked bark, framed a view right out past the breakers to the open sea.

'There was a ramshackle old cottage in that corner,'

Kate said, pointing. 'It had been there for years. It was only demolished quite recently.'

'The great Australian beach shack—that's quite a tradition,' he said. 'No doubt generations of the same family drove down from Sydney or Canberra to spend the long summer holidays on the beach.'

'I wouldn't get too nostalgic about it,' she said. 'It was very basic; just one step up from a shanty. I pitied the mum of the family having to cook in it on sweltering January days.'

'Maybe the guys barbecued the fish they'd caught.'

'You sound like you speak from experience. Did your family have a beach house when you were growing up?'

'We owned a beach house at Palm Beach—it's the most northern beach in Sydney.'

Her eyes widened. 'I know it—don't they call it the summer playground of the wealthy?'

'I guess they do,' he said. 'Our place was certainly no beach shack. And I never went fishing with my father. He was always at work.'

'Your mother?'

'She was partying.'

He shied away from the thinly veiled pity in Kate's eyes. 'Did you have brothers or sisters?' she asked.

He shook his head. 'I was an only child.'

As a little boy he had spent many lonely hours over the long school holidays rattling around the palatial house by himself. Then, when he'd turned fourteen, his father had started him working as a labourer on the company building sites during the holidays. It had been tough—brutal, in some ways, as the old hands had tested the 'silvertail' boss's son from the private school. But he'd been strong—both physically and mentally—and willing to prove himself. He'd won the doubters over.

From then on, the company had dominated his life. And he'd rarely gone back to that lonely Palm Beach house until he'd been old enough to take a group of his own friends.

'I envied the school friends who'd come back from a place like this full of tales of adventure.' He waved his hand towards the demolition site. 'I bet that old shack could have told some stories.'

'Perhaps. But only the one family got to enjoy the views and the proximity to the beach,' Kate said. She looked around the land with a distinctly proprietorial air. 'The owners got a good price for the land and now lots of people will be able to enjoy this magic place.'

'Spoken like a true, ruthless property developer,' he said, not entirely tongue-in-cheek. He had no issue with property developers—the good ones, that was—they were the company's lifeblood.

'I wouldn't say ruthless. More…practical,' she said with an uplifting of her pretty mouth.

'Okay. Practical,' he said.

'And don't forget creative. After all, no one else ever saw the potential of this land.'

'Okay. You're a practical and creative property developer without a ruthless bone in your body.'

'Oh, there might be a ruthless bone or two there,' she said with a flash of dimpled smile. 'But I wouldn't call me a property developer,' she said. 'I just like hotels.'

'Which is why we're standing here today,' he said. 'How did your interest come about?'

'When we were on tour with the dance company we stayed in some of the worst accommodation you could imagine.' She shuddered in her exaggerated, dramatic way that made him smile every time. Her face was so mobile; she pulled faces that on anyone else would be unattractive but on her were disarming.

'Let me count the ways in which we were tormented by terrible bedding, appalling plumbing and the odd cockroach or two. In one dump out west, we found a shed snakeskin under the bed.'

That made Sam shudder too. He hated snakes.

'Whenever we could manage it, a few of the girls and I scraped together the funds to lap up the luxury of a nice hotel where we lived the good life for a day or two.'

He nodded. 'I did the same thing in India. While we were working, we didn't expect accommodation any better than the people's homes we were rebuilding. When we were done, I checked in for a night at an extraordinary hotel in an old maharajah's palace.'

Her eyes sparkled green in the sunlight. 'Was it awesome? I would so love to see those Indian palace hotels.'

'The rooms were stupendous, the plumbing not so much. But I didn't care about that when I was staying in a place truly fit for a king.'

'That's it, isn't it? It doesn't have to be bandbox perfect for a good experience.' She bubbled with enthusiasm. 'It can be something more indefinable than gold-plated taps or feather mattresses. On those tours, I really got to know what made a good hotel or a bad one—regardless of the room rate. When the chance came to work with Ben at Harbourside, I jumped at it. I had to train from the ground up, but knew I'd found the career for me.'

'You've never wanted to work at a different hotel? A bigger one? Maybe somewhere else—one of those Indian hotels, perhaps? Or even Sydney?' He fought a hopeful note from entering his voice when he spoke about the possibility of her moving to his home city. There was no point. She was off-limits.

She shook her head emphatically. 'No. I want to work right here in Dolphin Bay. I couldn't think of anything else I would rather do than manage the new hotel. I want to make it the number-one destination on the south coast.'

She looked out to sea and he swore her dreams shone from her eyes.

But he was perturbed that her horizons seemed so narrow. In his view, she was a big fish in a small pond, too savvy to be spending her life in a backwater like this. And yet, despite that, her vision had been expansionary.

'What gave you the idea for this kind of resort?' he asked, genuinely interested.

She gave a self-deprecating shrug but he could tell she was burning to share her story. 'I saw friends flying to surf and yoga resorts in Bali. Others driving to Sydney to check in for pampering spa weekends. I wondered why people couldn't come to Dolphin Bay for that. We're well placed for tourists from both Canberra and Sydney: we've got the beach, we've got the beautiful natural environment. Get the eco credentials, and I reckon we could have a winner. Ben thought so too when I talked it over with him.'

'You've obviously done your research.' But as he thought about it, he realised there was something vital missing from her impassioned sell.

'You haven't actually visited the surf and spa hotels in Bali and Sydney yourself, by way of comparison?'

'Unfortunately, no.' Her face tightened and he could tell he'd hit a sore spot. 'I'm more of an armchair traveller. I know the best hotels' websites backwards, but I don't have the salary to afford overseas trips.'

He would enjoy showing her the world. The thought came from nowhere but with it the image of showing her some of the spectacular hotels he'd stayed in. Of taking her to the ones she'd dreamed of and ones she'd never imagined existed. But that went beyond the business brief of liaising on the hotel build.

'Maybe you should talk to Ben about your salary.' He couldn't imagine his old mate Ben would rip Kate off. But he knew only too well how tight-fisted some business people could be. His father had believed in rewarding people properly for their work and he'd followed suit. It was one of the reasons the company had so many loyal, long-serving employees.

Those people were why he hadn't immediately accepted the takeover offer. The owners of Lancaster & Son Construction had always prided themselves on being a family company, not only in the sense that it was owned by a family, but also because the people who worked for them were a family of sorts. Many of the staff would see a sale as a personal betrayal on his part. Worry about that was keeping him awake at night.

Kate shook her head. 'You probably know hospitality isn't the highest paying of industries, but Ben pays me fairly. And I've had the opportunity to learn the business from the ground up.'

'Soon you'll get the chance to see a hotel built from the ground up.'

'I can't wait to see it come to life,' she said, bubbling again with the enthusiasm he found so attractive.

She reached down for the clipboard she'd left on the bonnet of the small white van with the Hotel Harbourside logo. 'That's a cue to get down to business.'

'Fine by me,' he said. 'Fire away with any questions you might have.'

'Okay.' She looked up at him. 'Do I have to include the business questions in the questions I've got left with you?' She hastily amended her words. 'I mean, those questions wouldn't be about the actual building but about you. Uh… about you as our builder, I mean.'

'Fair enough,' he said. Her series of questions indicated

that underneath her businesslike attitude she might still be interested in him as a person, not just a contact. Though he doubted they'd be in one another's company long enough for her to ask them all.

'How long do you think it will take to build the resort?' she asked.

'From breaking ground to when you greet your first guests?'

She nodded.

'At least a year, maybe longer. This site is out of the way with a section of unsealed road to complicate matters in bad weather. That might pose problems with transporting equipment and materials. Then there's the fit-out to consider. You've specified a high standard of finish.'

'But you'll give us dates for commencement and completion in the final contract?'

'Of course. But we'll err on the side of conservative.' It was difficult to stay impartial and businesslike when the look of concentration on her face was so appealing; when the way she nibbled on the top of her pen made him want to reach over, pluck it from her hand and kiss her.

She scribbled some notes on her notepad. 'I'll include that in my report.'

Going on what he already knew about Kate, Sam had no doubt the report would be detailed and comprehensive.

'Talking like this makes it all seem very real,' she said. 'I'll be out here every day after work impatiently watching it go up. Will…will you be here to supervise it?'

He shook his head. 'There will be a construction manager on site. The team here will report back to Sydney.'

'So…you're just here for the one week?'

'That's right,' he said.

He wasn't sure whether he saw relief or disappointment in her eyes.

This was just one of many jobs for him but to her it was a big deal. He knew she wanted to do her best for Ben as well as make a mark for her own career. It would be best to be honest with her.

'Actually, there's a chance I won't be involved at all with the company by the time construction starts.' He kept his voice calm, not wanting to reveal the churning angst behind his words.

His obsession with the company had turned him into the worst kind of workaholic. Someone who, once his headspace was on the job, had pushed all other thoughts aside— family, friends, even his fiancée. His obsession had meant he had not been present at his father's deathbed. It had led his fiancée to dump him. To sell the company might free him to become a better person. But it could never be an easy decision.

Kate's eyes widened in alarm. 'What do you mean?'

'There's a serious offer on the table for the company.'

'You mean you're going to sell your family company?' The accusation in her eyes made him regret that he had opened the subject.

'It's an option. A decision I still have to make,' he said, tight-lipped.

She frowned. 'How could you do that when your father and grandfather built it up?' Her words stabbed like a knife in his gut. *Betrayal*—that was how people would see it. Like Kate saw it.

'Businesses are bought and sold all the time. You must know that.'

The words sounded hollow to his own ears. He knew what his father would have said—would have shouted, more like it. But he'd spent too many years trying to live up to his father's ambitions for him. The business was his now, to make the best deal as he saw it.

Her frown deepened. 'But surely not family concerns? It's…it's like the business has been entrusted to you, isn't it?'

What was she, the voice of his conscience?

'You could say that, but a company becomes an entity of its own,' he said. 'The multi-national company making the bid would grow it beyond what I could ever do in the current climate.'

'Bigger isn't always necessarily better, you know.'

He had no answer for that. Not when he couldn't understand why she wanted to lock herself away in a small town. But he *could* cut this conversation short, stop her from probing any further into the uncomfortable truths he had to deal with.

'That's beside the point,' he said. 'What I do with the company is my concern.'

Her mouth twisted. 'So you're telling me it's none of my business?'

'That's right,' he said.

Kate didn't know why she was shocked by Sam's revelation, or his blunt dismissal of the ensuing conversation. After all, her first impression of him was that he looked a tough, take-no-prisoners type of guy.

But then she'd seen a different side to his character with his talk of his volunteer work in India.

Who was the real Sam? Was she not the only one with lurking, unresolved issues?

She had to keep in mind he was a successful businessman. Could he have got where he was without elbowing other people aside, trampling over them, focusing only on the end goal no matter who might get hurt along the way?

But she didn't like the idea of him trampling over someone she cared about. 'What about Ben? That *is* my business. Ben trusts you to build this hotel. How could you be so…so disloyal to him?'

She didn't expect loyalty to her—after all, they were barely strangers—but the fact he could walk away so easily stung just a little.

His face was set rigid. 'There's nothing disloyal about it. It's business, pure and simple. Ben's a businessman himself, he'd understand that.'

'Don't be so sure of that. Ben wants you to build this hotel. Now I've met you, I…I want you to build the hotel. I call it disloyal if you hive it off to some other company we don't know.'

That scowl was back, his eyes bitter chocolate, dark and unreadable. 'Correction,' he said. 'You want the *company* to build your hotel. Not me personally.'

'That's not true. It's the personal connection that won you the tender.'

He towered above her. 'And I thought it was because of my expertise in building hotels.'

'That too, of course.' His glare made her fear she'd overstepped the mark. 'I'm sorry. I should back down.'

She was surprised that he didn't agree with her, remind her again it was none of her business. But she got the impression he carefully considered his next words. 'If—and it's still an "if"—the company is sold, the new owners will honour existing contracts and do exactly the same job as the company would have done under my direction.'

She exclaimed in disbelief. 'How can you say that? When our local deli was taken over by a bigger company, the first thing they did was sack people and the quality declined. Same thing happened with our garden centre. They were never the same. How can you be sure that wouldn't happen with your company?'

He paused. 'I can't be sure. If I sold, the new company would make certain assurances. But once new management was in charge they would do things their own way.'

'As I thought,' she said slowly. She dreaded having to bear this news to Ben.

'But as yet, I haven't made any decisions,' Sam said. 'That's one of the reasons I'm here, to take a break and think about the issue with a clear mind.'

Was that a crack in his armour of business speak?

'I still don't get it,' she said. 'Why would you consider selling, with all that family history invested in your company?'

'Try I'd never have to work again in my life?' His voice was strong and certain but the conviction was missing from his eyes.

She was probably totally out of line but she persisted. 'I don't know you very well, but I wonder if never working again would really satisfy you. What purpose would you have in life? I have the feeling you're not the kind of person who would be happy doing nothing.'

Sam's mouth tightened and his jaw tensed. She got the feeling she'd prodded a raw spot.

'Let me rephrase that,' he said. 'Selling would give me freedom to make my own mark, rather than carry on my father's vision for the company. To forge something new of my own.'

She paused. 'I guess there's that,' she said. She looked up at him. 'I might be speaking out of place here but—'

'But you're going to say it anyway,' he finished, with the merest hint of a smile that gave her the confidence to continue.

'Please think about it really carefully. Not just for Ben's

sake. Or mine. Or, I guess, the people who work for you. But for you.'

'I'll keep that in mind,' he said, his voice studiously neutral.

'Good,' she said. 'I don't know why, but I care about the effect it might have on you. You seem like a good person. And I reckon you might never forgive yourself if what makes your family company so special was to be destroyed.'

Sam swore under his breath. Every word Kate had said had hit home hard where he felt most vulnerable—and then hammered at his doubts and insecurities. How did she know how much he feared wrecking everything that was unique and good about his family company?

He'd known her for barely twenty-four hours yet straight away she seemed to have tuned in to the dilemmas that nagged at him regarding the sale. Yes, he'd seen moral outrage in those green eyes. But he'd also seen genuine understanding.

Frances, his ex-fiancée, would have advised sell, sell, sell. Not for the money, but to rid him of the business that she'd seen as a greedy mistress that had taken him too often from her side.

'You're a workaholic who doesn't care about anything but that damn company, and there's nothing left to give me.' Frances had said that on any number of occasions, the last when she'd flung her engagement ring at him. She'd never understood his compulsion to work that Kate had figured out within hours of meeting him. The compulsion he scarcely understood himself.

But he didn't welcome Kate's naive assumptions about the nature of the company deal. He didn't want to keep the business because of misplaced loyalty to an outmoded 'one set of hands on the steering wheel' management model. *He had to be one hundred per cent sure.*

'Thank you, Kate. You've made some good points and I'll certainly take them on board,' he said in a stiff, busi-nesslike tone. As if the deadline for his decision wasn't already making his gut churn and keeping him awake at night.

'I'm glad you're not offended,' she said. 'I don't want to get off to a bad start for our working relationship.' Her brows were drawn together in a frown and her eyes were shadowed with concern.

'Not offended at all. What you said makes sense. I'm not the type of guy who deals well with time on my hands. I like to be kept busy. A day out from the office and I'm getting edgy already.'

He had started to pace back and forward, back and for-ward, in the same few metres of ground in front of Kate. It was a habit of his when he was stressed. He was scarcely aware he was doing it.

In silence, she watched him, her head swivelling each time he turned, until eventually she spoke. 'Do you realise you're wearing a groove in the sand?'

He stopped. 'Just making a start on digging for the foundations,' he said in a poor attempt at defusing his embarrassment with humour. As a CEO, as the child of a dominant father who had expected so much of him, he didn't like revealing his weaknesses.

She stared at him for a long moment then laughed. 'Okay. I get it. But if this is what you're like when you're meant to be taking a break, I'd hate to see you when you're on a deadline,' she said.

He halted. 'I need to hit the gym. Or the surf. Get rid of some energy.'

'If you really want to keep busy, I have a job for you that could fill a few hours.'

'A job?'

She shook her head. 'No, sorry, forget I said anything. You don't like waste-of-time wedding things.' She looked up at him, green eyes dancing. 'Do you?'

CHAPTER SIX

SAM GRITTED HIS TEETH. Kate so obviously wanted him to cajole her into telling him about the job she wanted him to do. If he played along with her girly game he could end up with some ghastly wedding-related activity like tying bows on frilly wedding favours, or adding loops and curls to his no-nonsense handwriting on place cards—all activities he'd managed to avoid for his own cancelled wedding. On the other hand, if he called her bluff and didn't cajole her, he'd always wonder if it was a job he might have enjoyed, that would have helped take his mind of the looming deadline for his decision.

'Tell me what you'd like me to do and I—'

'Okay,' she said with delight. 'I'd like you—'

He put up his hand to stop her. 'Before you go any further, please let me finish. I reserve the right to pass on any excessively frivolous wedding duty.'

She pulled one of her cute faces. 'Oh dear. I'm not sure if what I was going to ask you to do would count as frivolous or not.'

He tapped his booted foot on the ground. 'Try me.'

She gave an exaggerated sigh. 'Okay, then. That wedding arch.'

'The wedding arch you thought I'd come here to build?'

'The very same. Only there was never a wedding arch. That was me jumping to conclusions.'

'But now there *is* a wedding arch.'

'The more I thought about it, the more I thought Sandy would love a wedding arch. And, as you told me you could build one, I thought it might be a good idea. As a surprise for the bride and groom.'

He shrugged. 'Why not?'

'You mean you'll do it?'

'Yep.'

'Really?' Her face lit up and for a moment he thought she was going to grab his hands for an impromptu jig, like she had last night. But then she turned away, aware, no doubt, as he was, that it was inappropriate behaviour for a business relationship.

He realised that, again, his devotion to the company and company rules was squashing the development of a potential relationship with a woman. Did it have to be that way? Was there a way he could keep the company and conquer the workaholic ways that had led him to be single at thirty when he had anticipated being happily married at this age? Maybe even with a family?

'But won't it be quite difficult?' she said. Kate's words brought him back to the present.

'For a simple wooden structure? Nah. I reckon I could get everything I need at your local hardware store. Just give me an idea of what you've got in mind.'

'I've looked on the Internet and downloaded some images of beautiful arches for inspiration. I'll show you on my phone.'

'Okay,' he said. He liked to work with his hands. He found the rhythm of sawing, sanding and painting relaxing. Kate's 'little job' might be just what he needed to get the takeover offer into perspective.

'But I'd have trouble getting flowers and ribbons at this stage,' she said.

He frowned. 'Ribbons?'

'Sorry, I'm thinking out loud,' she said.

'Do you need all that stuff? I can paint the arch white.'

'Nice. But not enough. Not for a wedding.' She thought some more. 'I've got it—lengths of white organza draped around the poles. Simple. Elegant. Sandy would love that.'

Sam wasn't too sure what organza was. 'That's some kind of fabric, right?'

'Yes. Fine, white wedding-like fabric.'

'Then we'll have to make sure the arch is anchored firmly in the sand. If it's windy we don't want the fabric to act like sails and pick it up.'

'Oh no. Can you imagine the whole structure taking off and flying into the ocean?' She gracefully waved her arms in her long white sleeves, miming wings, and he could see the dancer in her.

He had been dragged along with his mother to see *Swan Lake* for some charity function; he was struck by the image of Kate in costume as an exquisite white swan. He wished he'd seen her dance on stage.

'Yep. I can see the headlines in the *Dolphin Bay Daily*,' he said. '"Bridal Arch Lost at Sea".'

'Eek! Please don't tease me about it. A wedding planner's nightmare.' She frowned. 'That really would be a disaster, wouldn't it? Maybe we should forget the whole idea of the arch."

'I'll make it work. I promise.' He liked it that his words of reassurance smoothed away her frown.

'Thank you, Sam. You're being such a good sport about this.'

She looked up at him and smiled and there was a long moment of complicity between them.

Working on the project meant more time spent with Kate. He shouldn't be so pleased at the idea but he was. He usually looked temptation in the eye and vanquished it. Not so when it came to the opportunity to spend more time with this woman.

Building a wedding arch was the last thing he wanted to do. Correction—the frilly wedding favours would have been the last thing. But he'd happily make ten wedding arches if it meant seeing more of Kate. He couldn't have her. He couldn't date her. He couldn't think of her in terms of a relationship. But that wouldn't stop him enjoying her company in a hands-off way.

'Okay, now that you've reassured me it will work, I'm so excited we're doing this,' she said. 'I can't wait to see the look on Sandy's face when she walks onto the sand and sees it there.'

'Let's get on with it, then,' he said.

And try not to think about what it would be like to have a hands-on *relationship with Kate.*

'So, show me the pictures on your phone,' he said.

'Sure.' She burrowed into that oversized handbag and pulled out her phone. 'Here they are,' she said, holding it up. He moved towards her so he could stand behind her, looking over her shoulder to her phone. He ended up so close, if she leaned backward she would nestle against him, as if they were spooning. *Not a good idea.*

He took a step back but then he couldn't see. He narrowed his eyes. 'The sun's reflecting off the screen,' he said. 'All I can see is glare.' He reached around her shoulder so he could cup her phone with his hand and shade it from the sunlight.

Bad move. It brought him way too close to her. He had to fight to ignore his tantalising proximity to her slender back, the curves of her behind.

Was she aware too? Her husky voice got even huskier as she chattered on, which made him suspect she was not as unaware as she was trying to seem. 'This one's made with bamboo but I think it looks too tropical,' she said. 'I like the wooden ones best; what do you think?'

She scrolled through the images of fancy wedding arches, but he was finding it too hard to concentrate when he could only think of the way-too-appealing woman so close to him.

'Can you see it?' she asked, swaying back. Now they were actually touching. He gritted his teeth.

'Yes. The wooden one is good,' he said in a strangled voice.

'Might the bamboo be easier for you to make?' she said.

'The wooden is fine. Easy.'

'So you don't like the bamboo?'

'No.' He couldn't care less about the arch. He could easily look up some designs later himself when he got back to the hotel.

'Can you figure out the measurements you need?'

There was only one set of measurements on his mind, and it wasn't for a wooden wedding arch.

'You have to allow room for both bride and groom,' she nattered on, while he broke out in a cold sweat. 'Ben's tall, but Sandy isn't wearing a big skirt, so…'

He couldn't endure her proximity for a moment longer. 'I've got the measurements,' he said abruptly as he stepped back.

He wanted to forget every rule he'd ever made and gather her into his arms.

But he couldn't. She was a client. And, while he still owned the company, he still followed its rules. He was stuck here in Dolphin Bay until after the wedding. He had to get through his friend's ceremony without there being any awkwardness. Kissing Kate right now would be ill-advised. Unwise. Irresponsible.

And he just knew it would be utterly mind-blowing.

He took another step back so she was more than arm's length away, so he could not be tempted to reach out to her.

She turned to face him. 'Are you okay with that? Do you need to see more?' Her face was flushed, her eyes wide, her mouth slightly parted. *She felt it too.* He was sure she did. Maybe she was more disciplined than he was. Because all he wanted to do was kiss her. Claim that lovely mouth, draw her close to him.

'No. I've got it,' he said.

'So, now we've settled on the style we—I mean you—need to start making it happen.'

'I won't be able to do it by myself. You'll need to consult. Approve.'

The flush on her cheeks made her eyes seem even greener. 'Of course,' she said. 'If we want to keep the arch a secret, we'll have to work on it away from the bride and groom. There's a big shed at home. It…it used to be my father's; there are tools in there.'

'Sounds good,' he said.

'I'll give you the address and you can have the timber delivered there.'

She looked around her and then at her clipboard. 'Have we done all we need to do for the site inspection?'

'For the moment.'

'Let's go, then. I'll drop you at the hardware shop. I'll look for the organza but I don't think I'll find it in the quantity we'll need in any of the shops here. I might have to ask Sandy to get it for me in Sydney on Wednesday. I'll tell her it's for the table decorations. She won't question that.'

'Hold on,' Sam said. 'Why wouldn't you buy it in Sydney yourself?'

Kate stilled and didn't meet his gaze. 'Because I...I won't be going to Sydney.'

'What?' He was astounded. 'For the stag night? Hen night? Hag night? Whatever they're calling it.'

Her freckles stood out from her pale skin. 'No.'

'But you organised it.' He'd been looking forward to getting her on his home territory. He'd even been going to propose they all stay at his apartment instead of a hotel. He'd bought the large penthouse in anticipation of getting married. It was way too big for one person; sometimes he felt as lonely there as he had in the palatial Palm Beach house. Kate could have her own room; there would be no question of any more intimate arrangement.

She shook her head. 'I organised a night out in Dolphin Bay. Not Sydney.'

'You're upset that your plans were changed?'

Colour rushed back into her face. 'Of course not. If Lizzie can't come here, you should all go to Sydney. But not me, I'm afraid.'

He drew his brows together. 'I don't get it. Don't you want to be with your friends?' He paused. 'Is it because you don't want to spend time with Jesse? He's the best man. It would be difficult to avoid him.'

'No. Jesse and I are fine with each other now. It's as if the...the incident never happened. He's as relieved as I am.'

'I was going to suggest I show you around the Lancaster & Son headquarters while we're all in Sydney.'

'That would have been nice. Perhaps another time?'

The stubborn tilt of her chin and the no-nonsense tone of her voice made him realise she had no intention of coming to Sydney. To party, to visit his office, even for a change of scene.

'Sure,' he said. 'But this would be a good time for a visit to the office.'

'You mean while you still own the company?'

It felt painful to think there could very well be a time when he had no connection to the company. But how could he keep the business and stop making the mistakes that had blighted his life because of it?

'That too. But at the beginning of the job. You could meet the team who'll be working on the resort build. That way they won't be strangers when they come to Dolphin Bay.'

'By the time we got up to Sydney and back the next day, I'd be away for too long. I'm needed here.'

'At the hotel? Surely Ben can organise someone to replace you?'

'Maybe. But it's late notice. I'm also learning how to look after Sandy's bookshop while she's away on her honeymoon. I love Bay Books.'

Everything she loved seemed to be in Dolphin Bay.

He remembered how she'd referred to Sydney as 'outside'. It had seemed odd at the time.

'I can't believe Ben and Sandy would want you to stay here working and not go to Sydney with them. You're their bridesmaid.'

'It's not just them. I have…other commitments here.'

'Commitments?' He suddenly realised how little he knew about her. She could be a single mother with kids to support. She could have an illness that required regular hospitalisation. She could belong to some kind of sect that didn't allow partying. Who knew?

'I live with my mother and sister,' she said.

Okay, it was unusual to be living at home at twenty-eight years old, but not unheard of.

'And they don't let you leave town?' he quipped in a joke that immediately fell flat.

'Of course they do. I don't let myself leave town because I'm needed here.'

He frowned. He didn't think he was particularly obtuse but he didn't know what she was getting at. 'I don't follow you,' he said.

'My mother and I share the care of my sister,' she said. 'She was injured in a car crash when she was eleven and left a paraplegic. She's confined to a wheelchair.'

For a long moment, Sam was too stunned to speak. That was the last thing he had anticipated. 'I'm sorry,' he eventually managed to say.

'No need to apologise,' said Kate. 'You weren't to know. Mum's a nurse and often works night shift at the Dolphin Bay Community Hospital. My sister, Emily, says she's fine on her own, but we like to be there when we can.'

'I understand,' he said.

Did he really? Sometimes Kate didn't understand herself how she'd ended up at her age living at home with her mother and her twenty-six-year-old sister.

Sam's brow was furrowed. 'But you lived in Sydney and travelled with your dance troupe. Who looked after your sister then?'

She wished he wouldn't ask the awkward questions that made her look for answers she didn't want to find. The more he spoke, the more she could see herself reflected in his eyes. And she wasn't sure she was at ease with what she saw.

'My mother. Then she broke her arm, couldn't manage and asked could I come home for a while.'

'How long ago was that?'

'Five years ago.' Right when she'd fallen apart after the near-assault and had left the dance troupe. She'd been glad for an excuse to run home.

'And you never left again?'

'That's right.'

'That's when you started to work for Ben?'

'Yes. Though it was only casual hours at first. You see, I'd dropped out of university in the final year of my business degree.'

'To join the dance troupe?'

'Yes.' There'd been so much more to it than that. But she wasn't ready to share it with Sam. With anyone. 'So when I came back, I finished my degree part-time at a regional campus not far from here.'

'And here you've stayed.'

'Put like that it sounds so grim. Trust me, it isn't. I'm happy here. This is a fabulous community to live in. And I love my job.' She tried not to sound overly defensive.

'If you say so.' He didn't look convinced. Who would blame him? Even her mother urged her to get more of a life. 'I'm not one for small towns,' he said.

'Dolphin Bay might not be for everyone but it suits me.'

'Sure,' he said. 'But I'm sorry you're not coming to Sydney for the party. Have you told Sandy?'

She shook her head. 'No, I haven't, and I'd appreciate it if you didn't tell her. I'll make an excuse at the last minute so she doesn't waste time trying to convince me to change my mind. Because I won't.'

'*I* can't make you change your mind?'

If anyone could, it would be him. 'Not even you.'

The knots of anxiety that could tie her up for hours were starting to tighten. She could lose control. She had to stop thinking about the trip to Sydney, not get caught up in that vortex of fear.

But right now she had to be cheerful Kate and put a bright face on it.

'Let's get moving, then, shall we? We've got a top-secret wedding arch to build.'

CHAPTER SEVEN

SAM NOTICED THREE things about the home Kate shared with her mother and sister as he approached it the next afternoon. The first was the wheelchair-friendly ramps that ran from the street to the house. The second was the riotously pretty garden and tubs of bright flowers everywhere. The third was the immediate sense of warmth and welcome that enveloped him when Kate opened the door to him.

'Come in,' she said with a smile that sparkled with dimples. 'The delivery from the hardware store has arrived. I got them to stack it in the shed out the back.'

She had only recently finished her shift at the hotel but had already changed into faded jeans and a snug-fitting T-shirt. The simple clothes did nothing to hide her shapely body. That was going to prove distracting. And yet even if she were dressed in an old sack he'd find her distracting.

It was getting more difficult with every moment he spent with Kate to think of her only as a business contact. He shoved his hands in his pockets so he wouldn't be tempted to greet her with a hug.

Inside, the open-plan house was nothing special in architectural terms, comfortably furnished with well-worn furniture in neutral colours. What made it stand out was that it had obviously been redesigned to accommodate a wheelchair—plenty of space left between furniture and the kitchen benches set much lower than was usual.

Framed photographs propped on practically every surface caught his eye: a wedding photo from thirty-odd years ago, baby photos—the adorable infant with the fuzz of ginger hair and gummy smile with tiny dimples already showing must surely have been Kate. There was another of Kate wearing a checked school uniform with her wayward hair tamed into two thick plaits. Kate with her arm around a younger girl with strawberry-blond hair. Kate, graduating in a cap and gown.

But the picture that held his attention was a large, framed colour photograph hanging on the wall of a young Kate in a classical ballet costume. The slender teenager was wearing a white dress with a tight, fitted bodice with gauzy wings at the back and a full translucent skirt. She balanced on pointed toes in pink ballet slippers. Her pale graceful arms were arched above her head to frame her face. Her hair was scraped right back off her face but glowed with fiery colour, and her green eyes sparkled with irrepressible mischief.

Sam gestured to it. 'That's nice.'

'When I was thirteen I was embarrassed when Mum hung it up so prominently. Now I look at that girl and think she was kinda cute.'

Sam's mother didn't like family photos cluttering up the house. There was just one of him as a baby framed in heavy silver on her dressing table. There had been photos of him in the formal blazer and striped tie of his private school, others of him playing football. They used to be in his father's study. He had no idea where they were now. He was gripped by a sudden, fierce desire to get them back. One day, when he had his own family, he wanted the living room to look like this one—not the stark, empty elegance of his mother's.

'You were lovely,' he said, then quickly amended, '*Are* lovely.'

'Thank you,' she said, looking wistfully at the photo. 'It seems so long ago now. I thought I was going to be a prima ballerina. So much has happened since.'

The time the photo was taken must have been around the time she'd shared her first kiss with Jesse. Again jealousy seared him. Unwarranted, he knew; he had no reason to doubt Jesse or Kate. Jesse had taken him aside and explained that, while he loved Kate like a sister, there was absolutely no romance between them. But still he felt uncomfortable at the thought of them kissing.

There was another equally large framed photo of an attractive, strawberry-blond teenager playing wheelchair basketball. 'Is this your sister?' She was holding the ball up ready to shoot a goal with strong, muscular arms, her expression focused and determined.

'Yes. Emily's a champion basketball player.'

He looked around the room. 'She's not home now?'

'No. She's an accountant at the bank in Dolphin Bay, so won't be home until this evening. Though you might meet Mum; she'll be knocking off from the hospital early today.'

'I'll look forward to that,' he said. He was curious about the dynamic between three adult women sharing a house.

'Come on,' said Kate. 'I'll take you out the back to the shed. I'm looking forward to getting started on the *amazing arch*.' She said the last two words with typical Kate exaggeration.

'So it's to be an *amazing* arch now, is it?' he asked as he followed her.

'Of course. After all, you're making it,' she said with that unconsciously flirtatious lilt to her husky voice.

'I'm flattered you're so confident in my abilities,' he said.

She laughed but, as she neared the old wooden shed at the bottom of the garden, her laughter trailed away. She stopped outside the door. 'I…I don't go in here often.'

'You said it was your father's workshop. He's not around?'

Kate looked straight ahead rather than at him. 'He…he was driving the car when Emily was injured. Another car was on the wrong side of the road. Dad swerved to avoid a head-on collision but smashed into a tree.'

For a long moment Sam was too shocked to speak. 'I'm sorry.'

'Emily was trapped inside the car. He…Dad…walked away uninjured. But Emily… Her spine was broken.' Kate's mouth twisted. 'Dad never forgave himself. Couldn't deal with it. Started drinking. Eventually he…he left. Six months later, he died.'

Sam found it hard to know what to say as Kate's family tragedy unfolded. 'When did that happen?'

Her arms were tightly folded across her chest. 'The accident happened not long after that photo of me at my ballet concert was taken.'

'That must have been tough for you.' He knew the words were inadequate but they were the best he could come up with. He had lost his father but it had been to a quick heart attack. He'd gone too soon, and he still mourned him, but the loss hadn't been in the tragic way of Kate's father.

She nodded. 'For me. For my mum. Most of all for Emily. She was in hospital for more than a year. Our lives changed, that's for sure.'

He longed to reach out and draw her into his arms but couldn't bring himself to do it. It would change things between them and he didn't know that she would want that. Or if he did.

Instead he pushed open the door to the shed. Inside it was neat and orderly. Hand tools were arranged on shadow boards. Nails and screws were lined up by size in old glass jars. He whistled his appreciation. 'This is a real man cave. Your dad must have liked spending time here.'

Kate hesitated, only one foot past the doorway. 'He liked making things. Fixing things. I…I spent lots of time in here with him. He taught me how to be a regular young handywoman.'

Just as his father had decided to make a man of him and introduce him to building sites.

Kate adept with hammer and saw? She continued to surprise him. 'That's a good attribute in a girl.'

'He wanted me to grow up as an independent woman who didn't need a man to change a tap washer for her.'

'And did you?'

'He left before he completed my workshop education.' Her voice was underlined with a bitterness he hadn't heard from her before.

'I'm sorry,' he said again. He realised that while he could handle disputes on building sites, or argue the fine points of a multi-million-dollar contract, he was ill-equipped to deal with emotion. Frances had accused him of being so tied up with the company he couldn't care about anything—or anyone—else. Perhaps she'd been right.

'He changed so much,' said Kate. 'Changed towards me. Became angry when he'd always been so even-tempered. I was okay, he was okay, but Emily was lying broken in her hospital bed. Survivor's guilt, I suppose now. But as a kid I didn't know about all that. In a way…in a way I was glad when he went.'

Sam stood silent, not knowing how to comfort her in her still-present grief, raging at himself that he couldn't. He was relieved when she changed the subject.

'Anyway, enough about that,' she said with a forced cheerfulness to her voice. We've got an *amazing* wedding arch to make.'

Kate found it disconcerting to have another man working in her father's shed—and totally distracting because the man was Sam in jeans, work boots and a white T-shirt. Strong, capable and utterly male.

For a moment it seemed like the past and present collided. Yesterday, she was the little girl revelling in being allowed to work with Daddy in his shed, her father kind and endlessly patient. Today the grown-up Kate was acutely aware of tall, broad-shouldered Sam dominating the restricted space. Sam, the successful—and possibly ruthless—businessman. Sam, the man who spent his vacation helping people in need. Sam, who had been so good-natured about agreeing to make the arch she was sure would delight her friends on their special day.

Her dad would have liked him.

She forced the thought away. For so long, her memories of her father had been bitter ones. Not that he had caused Emily's accident—his action in the car had saved her sister's life—but the way he had changed afterward. Had become someone so different he had frightened her.

But being here with Sam was bringing back the happy memories, memories of being loved and cherished.

Sam checked the delivery from the hardware store. 'It's all here,' he said. He looked around him. 'Your dad had a good collection of tools. That orbital saw is in good nick. I'd like to use it.'

'Help yourself,' she said. 'And anything else you need. Nobody else uses the tools.'

'Not even you? Not after what your father taught you?'

'No,' she said, her tone letting him know she didn't want to talk any further about her father.

She stepped back from Sam, though there wasn't much room to move in the confined space of the shed. Wherever she stood, she wasn't far from him. She was aware of his proximity, the way his muscles flexed as he hauled the timber into place, the way he looked so good in those jeans.

She liked the assured way he handled the pieces of timber as he showed her how he intended to construct the arch. 'There will be four sturdy supports and four corresponding brace supports across the top,' he explained, running his hands along the length of the timber. 'Building it with four supports instead of just two will make it much more stable.'

His hands were large and well-shaped, strong but deft. She refused to let herself think about how they would feel cradling her face, stroking her body...

'Tell me where you want to drape your fabric and I'll insert a series of pegs you can wind it around to keep it in place,' he said.

'That sounds perfect,' she said. 'Clever you.'

'The actual structure will be quite big and cumbersome,' he said. 'I'm going to use hinges so we can easily dismantle it to get it to the beach in your van and put it together again.'

'Good idea,' she said. 'We'll have to work on the logistics of that. Like, when do I attach the fabric, and how do we get it to the beach early enough so it's a surprise? We might have to let someone else in on the secret.'

Sam paused and looked searchingly at her. 'Have you spoken to Sandy about getting the fabric yet?'

She couldn't meet his gaze. 'I'll do that tomorrow.'

'Are you sure you won't change your mind about going to Sydney?'

'No,' she said firmly so he wouldn't be aware of the fear thudding through her at the thought of getting in a car and driving to Sydney. 'As I said, it's too inconvenient.'

'You'll be letting your friends down—'

She spoke over him. 'Don't you think I know that?' She wanted her voice to sound firm, even a little angry, at his interference but it came out shaky and unsure.

She turned her back on him and picked up one of her father's pliers from the shadow board. She remembered it was one of his favourite tools and hung it back again on the exact spot where he had so carefully outlined its shape.

She tried to avoid the empty section of shadow board where her set of child-sized tools had hung. Her dad had bought them for the birthday she'd turned eleven. After he'd left, in a fit of anger and grief she'd pulled them down and hurled them to the ground, wanting to destroy them. She didn't know what had happened to them after that.

'I see where you got your organisational skills from,' Sam said in a voice that was too understanding.

A voice that made her want to rest her head on his broad shoulder and confess how confused and scared she was. Tell him she didn't know what was wrong with her, that she was letting her friends down. How she was dreading letting Sandy know she wouldn't be going to Sydney.

Instead, she pasted on her bright, cheery smile and turned back to face him.

'Can I tell you again how much I appreciate you doing this for me?' she said.

'You're welcome,' he said gruffly and she knew she hadn't fooled him one bit. 'Now you've told me your dad taught you some handywoman skills, I guess I can count on you to help.'

'I'm not that great with saws or drills. But I can hammer and use a screwdriver, and I'll put my hand up for sanding.

I'm very good at sanding.' She picked up a sanding block from the bench to prove the point. 'The surface will have to be really smooth. We don't want Sandy's gown catching on it and snagging. Can't have a bride with a snagged gown—not on my watch.'

She was aware she was speaking too rapidly. Aware that it wasn't just from nervousness but acute awareness of Sam—his perceptive brown eyes that saw right through to her innermost yearnings; the heat of his powerfully muscled body that warmed her even without them touching. Just looking at his superb physique and so handsome face made her feel wobbly at the knees.

Towering above her, he seemed to take up every bit of the confined space. When he took a step closer it brought him just kissing distance away. She would only have to reach out her hand to stroke that scar on his eyebrow that she found so intriguing, to trace the high edge of his cheekbone, to explore with trembling fingers his generous, sensual mouth.

Looking intently into her face, and without saying a word, he took the block from her suddenly nerveless fingers and placed it on the bench. 'No need for that right now,' he said. Her breath caught in her throat in a gasp that echoed around the walls of the small space.

She didn't resist when, without another word, he drew her close, cupped her chin in his hand and kissed her. She sighed with pleasure and kissed him right back, her heart tripping with surprise, excitement and anticipation. Hadn't she wanted this from the day she'd first seen him?

His lips were firm and warm and, when his tongue slipped into her mouth, passion—so long dormant—ignited and surged through her. She quickly met his rhythm with her own, slid her hands up to rest on his broad shoulders, delighted in the sensation of their closeness.

This was how a kiss should be. This kiss—Sam's kiss—consigned any other kiss she'd ever had into oblivion.

His breath was coming fast and so was hers. Desire, want, need: they all melded into an intoxicating hunger for him.

He pulled her close to his hard chest and his powerful arms held her there, her soft curves pressed against him. His kiss became harder, more demanding, more insistent. She thrilled to the call of his body and her own delirious response.

They kept on kissing. But the force of his kiss pushed her backwards against the wall of the shed so it pressed hard into her back with no way of escaping the discomfort. Suddenly her mind catapulted her back to the farmer forcing his unwanted attentions on her. He'd backed her into a boot cupboard, confined, airless—like the shed she was in now.

Sudden fear gave her the strength to put her hands flat against Sam's chest and push him away. 'No!' she cried. He released her immediately.

Swaying, she gripped on to the edge of the bench beside her.

His breathing came fast and heavy; her own was so ragged she could barely force out words. 'I'm sorry. I'm so sorry, I—'

'I rushed you,' he said hoarsely.

'No. It wasn't that. Things moved so quickly. I was… scared.'

He drew his dark brows together in a frown. 'Scared? I would never hurt you, Kate.'

'I…I know that. It's just…' There was no easy explanation for her behaviour.

'Just what? Is there something wrong?' His voice was rich with concern, which only made her feel worse.

'No. Nothing wrong,' she lied. But she knew she should tell him that it was nothing he'd done. That it was old fears, old hurts, that were tethering her. 'Sam, I—'

At that moment her mobile phone rang. She picked it up and swore silently at the voice of the panicking staff member at the other end. She put the phone back in her bag and turned to Sam, unable to meet his eyes.

'Th…there's an emergency at the hotel they seem to think only I can solve.' She didn't know whether to be relieved or annoyed at the interruption.

'Go,' he said.

'What just happened—I'm sorry.'

'Nothing to be sorry about,' he said. 'You're needed at work. You have to be there. No one knows that better than I do. Work comes first. It…it always has with me.' There was an edge to his voice that made her wonder what was behind those words. Again she wondered if she wasn't the only one with secret hurts in her past.

'Are you sure you'll be okay here?'

'Sure. It will be good to get stuck into working on the arch. I want to get as much as I can done before I leave for Sydney tomorrow.'

Saying goodbye was awkward. Now there could be no denying their mutual attraction. They were not friends, so no casual kiss on the cheek. Not just business contacts, so shaking hands would be inappropriate.

The kisses they'd shared had changed everything, had broken the barrier of business that they had constructed between them and had left her wanting more kisses—wanting *more* than kisses. But she'd freaked out and pushed him away. What must Sam think of her?

The emergency at work took longer than Kate expected. The glitch in the online reservation system had required rather more than the tweak she'd initially thought. It was more than two hours later before she returned home. She headed for the shed but was disappointed to find it empty.

The pieces of timber Sam had been working on lay across her father's pair of old wooden sawhorses. Wood shavings and sawdust had fallen to the floor and their sharp fragrance permeated the room. Sam's leather work gloves, moulded to the shape of his hands, sat on the bench top. She picked one up. It still felt warm from his body heat. She couldn't resist the temptation to put it to her face and breathe in the scent of the leather and Sam. It was intoxicating.

Where was he? She was surprised at the depth of her disappointment that he hadn't waited for her. Had her reaction to his kiss made him leave?

Her mobile phone rang from her handbag. Her mum. 'We heard you come in. Sam's in the house with me and Emily.'

Of course.

Why hadn't she realised that would happen? She'd told her mother that Sam would be using the shed. Mum, in her hospitable way, would have popped in to see how he was and next thing she'd probably have invited him in for a cup of tea.

Sam looked quite at home on the sofa drinking tea, as predicted, with her mother and Emily. His big boots were propped by the door and he was in socked feet. She drank in the sight of him, looking so relaxed and at ease in her home. Her heart seemed to swell with the pleasure of it.

'Sorry, I got held up, Sam,' she said.

He immediately got up to greet her. His eyes connected with hers, probing, questioning. But his voice was lighthearted. 'As you can see, I'm being well looked after. Dawn's chocolate fudge cake is the ideal fuel for a hungry man.'

There was a tiny smear of chocolate on the top of his lip that she found endearing. She fought the impulse to lean over and wipe it off with her finger. Tried to fight the thought of what it might be like to lick it off, then follow it with a kiss that would show him how much she wanted him and negate the awkwardness of their earlier encounter.

'Sam was working so hard out there, I thought he needed feeding,' said her mother.

'Thanks, Mum,' she said. 'You always think people need feeding.'

'You mean you're going to pass on a piece of chocolate cake?' said her mother.

'Of course not,' Kate said, affecting horror. 'Bring it on, please.'

'Sam's been filling us in on your project,' said Emily. 'I love the idea of the wedding arch.' She laughed. 'Sandy's plan to have just her and Ben and Hobo on the beach with no one else sure isn't going to happen.'

'It will still be simple and intimate, but with just a few more guests and a lot more to eat afterwards,' said Kate, unable to prevent the defensive note that crept into her voice.

'Sandy won't regret it,' said Dawn. 'Your wedding day should be something really special you can always look back on with joy. Sandy will thank you, sweetie, for taking it in hand for her.'

'Did you say Hobo was going to be part of the wedding?' asked Sam. 'You mean Ben's dog?'

As a guest at Hotel Harbourside, he would be familiar with the big, shaggy golden retriever who was often to be found near the reception desk.

'Yes,' said Kate. 'He'll be wearing a wide, white bow around his neck.'

'If he doesn't chew it off first,' said Emily.

'How well trained is Hobo?' asked Sam. 'I'm thinking about the arch.'

'Oh no, you don't think he...?'

Sam shrugged. There was a definite twinkle in those dark eyes. 'Dogs and lamp posts. Dogs and trees. Why not dogs and wedding arches?'

Kate stared at him. 'Noooo! Hobo lifting his leg on our beautiful wedding arch in the middle of the ceremony? Not going to happen. Someone will have to make darn sure he stays on his leash.'

'Another job for the wedding planner,' said Sam. 'Better appoint an official dog minder and write them out a schedule of duties.'

There was a moment of silence. Kate saw her mother and Emily exchange glances. Did they really think she would take offence at Sam's teasing?

Emily laughed, which broke the tension. 'Sam, have you ever got Kate sussed out already.'

Her mother laughed too, then Sam, and Kate joined in. It was warm, friendly, inclusive laughter.

'Kate, we've invited Sam to stay for dinner,' said Dawn. 'If that's okay with you.'

Sam caught her eye. She could see he liked being here, liked her family. But he was waiting for her to give her okay. Had the kiss they'd shared made any difference?

'That's fine by me,' she said.

But she knew she'd have to be on guard all evening. Their passionate encounter had made a difference to her. She could no longer deny how strongly she was attracted to him. And she knew beyond a doubt she was in serious danger of developing deeper feelings for Sam.

CHAPTER EIGHT

TELLING SANDY SHE wouldn't be going to Sydney for the bridal party's night out was every bit as difficult as Kate had dreaded it would be. And then some.

Kate cringed at the hurt in her friend's eyes. Her excuses for why she was dropping out of the trip were weak and didn't stand up well to interrogation.

'I totally don't believe Emily needs you to be here with her tonight,' Sandy said.

Neither would her fiercely independent, mobile sister if she'd known she'd been used as an excuse. In fact, Emily would be furious.

'Is this about Sam?' Sandy asked. 'Are you mad at me and Ben for throwing you together with him?'

'Not at all. I really like him. Seriously, I do.' The cursed blush crept into her cheeks.

'Then *why?*'

I don't know! Tell me and we'll both know.

Kate bit down on her bottom lip to stop it from betraying her with an about-to-cry quiver. She felt so bad about letting Sandy down. But she'd suffered enough humiliation over the Jesse disaster not to want anyone—even Sandy—to know she couldn't even explain to *herself* why she was staying behind.

'I'm sorry but I just can't go. Can we leave it at that?'

Sandy eventually gave up her questioning. But Kate felt more and more miserable by the minute.

The wedding party had decided to go up to Sydney in one car. Kate stood in the driveway of Hotel Harbourside, perilously close to tears, as she watched Sam throw his overnight bag into the boot of Ben's big SUV.

Just as she thought he was about to leave, Sam turned and strode towards her. 'Last chance. Are you sure you won't come with us?' he said in a voice lowered for her ears only.

There was nothing she wanted more than to go with him. To throw herself into his arms and say 'yes.' But she was terrified of what might happen when she tried to get into the car.

Poor Kate.

In her mind, she could hear the shocked exclamations as if they were really happening.

No way would she ruin this moment for her friends, or endure further humiliation for herself.

She looked back up at Sam and mutely shook her head.

He met her gaze for a long moment, then frowned, obviously perplexed by her behaviour. 'Okay,' he said and turned away. 'I'll see you tomorrow when we get back.' He made no attempt to touch her, to kiss her goodbye. But then why would he, when she had so soundly rejected his last kiss?

Would he ever want anything to do with her again?

Shoulders slumped, she watched him head to the car. Ben and Sandy sat in the front and Sam climbed in with Jesse in the back. If she'd gone with them, would they have expected her to sit in the middle between Sam and Jesse? She wouldn't have let that happen. She would have wanted it to be just her and Sam.

As the car pulled away from the hotel driveway she

turned her back on it and dragged one foot after the other, away from the hotel. No way did she want to wave them off. She wished she could have gone with them to celebrate the wedding of two people she cared about, who both deserved their second chance at happiness.

But something she didn't understand was holding her back with a grip she seemed powerless to resist. She knew what would have happened if she'd tried to get into that car—pounding heart, nausea, limbs paralysed.

What was wrong with her?

She left the hotel behind her and kept walking, away from the harbour and along the boardwalk that led to Big Ray beach.

Had she become such a small-town hick she'd developed an aversion to fast traffic and bright lights?

She walked slowly along the beach, mid-week quiet with only a few people enjoying the surf, not taking her usual joy from the sight of the aquamarine water. She didn't even look out for the big, black manta rays for which the beach had been unofficially named.

At the north end of the beach, where the sand ended, she clambered over the rocks that divided Big Ray from the next beach. It was low tide and the rocks were fully exposed, smelling of salt and seaweed and the occasional whiff of decay from some poor stranded sea creature. She climbed down the final barrier of rocks onto the sand of the neighbouring beach, Wild Water, which had waves so violent and rips so dangerous only the boldest of adolescent surfers braved its waters.

Was it because she feared being alone with Sam?

With the rocks behind her, ahead of her was a stretch of white sand, bounded by rocks again at its northern end. To her right was the vast expanse of the Pacific Ocean. To her left was the freshwater river with its clear, cool water.

She slipped off her sandals and scuffed her feet in the sandbar that blocked the estuary of the river from flowing into the sea. The sandbar had appeared after the last big storm to hit the coast. It would just as likely disappear in the next one. In the meantime, the thwarted river pooled into a wide stretch of safe, shallow water. Her parents had taught her and Emily to swim here. She remembered again her father's endless patience and encouragement.

On one side were sand dunes, on the other bush straggled down a slope right down to the banks of the river, stands of spotted eucalypts reflected in the still waters of the lagoon. The beach bordered national park and there wasn't a building in sight. Sometimes kangaroos came down to the surf and splashed in the shallows, much to the delight of visitors, but there weren't any today.

This was one of her very favourite places. When she'd been on tour, tossing and turning in yet another uncomfortable hotel bed, she'd closed her eyes and envisaged its peace and beauty. In the first rapturous weeks of her romance with R—she could only bear to think of him by his initial—she'd told him about this place and suggested he come with her to see it. Thankfully he had scorned the idea, and that meant it was untainted by memories of him.

She inhaled a deep breath of the fresh salt-tangy air. And another. And another. Somehow she had to get herself together. If she couldn't get her thoughts in order here, she couldn't anywhere.

Dolphin Bay was her safe place. This place was her safest of the safe. But had she somehow transformed a safe place into a trap from which she could never escape?

Sam sat in the back seat of Ben's car, headed north to Sydney on the Princes Highway. There should have been laughter and banter as they started to celebrate in time-honoured style Ben and Sandy's last nights of 'freedom' from matrimonial chains.

But an uncomfortable silence had fallen upon the car. Kate.

No one wanted to mention her. No one wanted to express their worries about why their friend had reneged on part of the wedding arrangements she had so wholeheartedly thrown herself into. He, who had known her for such a short time, was eaten up with concern about her.

How had she become so important, so quickly?

The car passed the last petrol station on the far outskirts of town.

'Stop the car,' Sam said. 'Can you pull over here, please, Ben?'

Ben did as directed, bringing the car to a halt on the side of the road.

'Do you need to visit the little boy's room, mate?' asked Jesse.

'No,' said Sam. 'I'm going back for Kate.'

The sound of the combined intake of three sets of breath echoed through the interior of the car.

'Good,' said Sandy at last. She twisted around from the front seat to face Sam. 'There's something wrong. I'm worried about her. Really worried.'

'Me too,' said Jesse. 'It's unlike Kate to pass on the chance of a party.'

'She wouldn't come to Sydney with me to help me choose my wedding dress, either,' added Sandy. 'At the time I thought she wanted me to have time just with Lizzie. Now I'm not so sure that was her reason.'

'Should we all go back?' asked Ben.

'No,' said Jesse. 'It should be Sam. When it comes to Kate, Sam's the man.'

As he got out of the car, Sam nodded to Jesse in unspoken male acknowledgement of what his words had meant.

'Tell her how much we want her to come,' Ben called after him. 'Kate's been so good to us. It won't be the same without her.'

Sam didn't have to wait long to hitch a ride back into town. Once back at the hotel he dumped his bag and went to look for Kate. Her mobile went to voice mail. Neither her mother nor sister answered the phone at their home. Finally, the girl at the hotel reception told him Kate wasn't on duty but that, after the boss and his fiancée had taken off for Sydney, she had seen her heading in the direction of the beach.

Sam strode out towards the boardwalk to Big Ray beach. The surf beach was practically deserted. He spied a lone set of small, female-looking footprints just above the waterline. The footprints tracked along the length of the beach right to the end where the rocks took over. Shallow, swirling waves were encroaching and starting to obliterate them. He remembered Kate telling him about the idyllic place she loved on the next beach. The footprints turned out slightly, ballet-dancer style. He took a punt they were hers.

Kate sat in the shade of a grove of overhanging gum trees set back from the water's edge. She wished she could have a swim but the one thing her capacious handbag didn't hold was a swimsuit. When she was younger she wouldn't have hesitated to strip off her dress and swim in her underwear in the welcoming waters of the lagoon. She would even swim nude on a day like this when there wasn't another soul in sight.

She wouldn't risk that now, not since R had insinuated into her psyche such doubts about her body, her sexuality, her desires. Not since her attacker had taunted her about her provocative dance moves and her immodest stage outfits.

These days she kept everything buttoned up: her emotions, her desires, her needs. She realised, with a sharp stab of despair, that she had barricaded herself against intimacy, against love, against feeling.

Against allowing herself to admit the depth of her attraction to Sam and enjoy to the full the pleasure of being in his arms.

She sat hunched over with her arms wrapped around her knees, lost in the thoughts that spun around and around in her brain. How had she come to this, sitting alone on a beach, when the life she wanted went on around her?

When she was younger the restrictions of small-town life had chafed her. She'd thought the best view she'd ever see of Dolphin Bay would be in the rear-view mirror as she'd left to go to university in Sydney. Back then, she'd been full of hope and ambition and dreams of seeing the world. She'd never imagined she'd come back to Dolphin Bay as anything other than a visitor to catch up with her family and old friends.

She shut her eyes. The muted rhythm of the waves crashing on the nearby sand was near-hypnotic. A breeze gently rustled the branches of the trees above her. It was like she was going deep inside herself to dark places she had never wanted to see again. Deep. Deep. Deeper.

She didn't know how much time had elapsed before the sound of dried twigs crunching underfoot and a shadow falling across her made her snap back out of the trance and her eyes flew open.

She blinked at the light and then focused on the unexpected intruder in her solitary reverie.

'Sam? What are you doing here?' She shook her head

to clear her thoughts, pasted on her best smile. 'This is a surprise.'

He smiled back—that heart-wrenchingly wonderful smile—as he towered above her, his strong, muscular legs planted firmly in the sand. 'What did I want to go to Sydney for? I live there. I can party in the city any old time.' He'd rolled up his jeans; he was barefoot.

'But...I saw you leave with the others...'

He shrugged. 'So I came back. I thought I'd rather stay in Dolphin Bay and count the seagulls—or whatever you do for fun in this part of the world.'

In spite of herself, she giggled. 'Stay still for a moment and you might see a goanna running up a gum tree. That's nearly as much fun.'

'Yeah. Right,' he said with a grin. 'I forgot to tell you, I don't care much for reptiles, especially huge lizards.'

'So you just happened to come upon me here?' she said. Her heart leapt at the thought he might have sought her out.

'I remembered you told me about this place when I asked you about good spots to swim. I figured I might like to see it for myself.'

'So where's your swimsuit and towel?' she said in mock interrogation.

'If I hadn't encountered a certain redhead, I'd planned on diving in without the benefit of swimsuit or towel.'

She couldn't help a swift intake of breath at the thought of Sam stripping off his clothes and plunging naked into the water. She had to mentally fan herself. 'Oh, really?' she said when she thought her voice would work again.

He threw up his hands in surrender. 'Okay. You got me. I came back for you.' His tone was light-hearted but his eyes were very serious.

'For me?' Her heart started to thud at twice its normal rate.

Now he dropped all pretence at levity. 'To see if I could talk you into driving with me to Sydney. Just you and me. We could join the others later.'

'Why would you do that when I'm just…just a business contact?'

He looked down at her and for a long, still moment their gazes connected so there was scarcely a need for words. 'I think you know we're more than that,' he said finally.

'Yes,' she said. 'I believe I knew that from the get-go.'

She went to get up but she'd been sitting in the same position for so long, her right foot had gone numb and she stumbled. He caught her by both hands and pulled her to her feet. When she regained her balance, he kept hold of her hands. She was intensely aware of his nearness, his scent, his strength. There was no terror, no overwhelming urge to break free from his hold. Not in this safe place. Not with Sam.

'Wh…what did the others think about you coming back for me?'

'They couldn't understand why you didn't want to go with them.'

She gasped and the gasp threatened to turn into a sob. 'Sam, can't you see it's not that I don't *want* to go to Sydney? It's that I *can't.*'

She tried to twist away from him, embarrassed for him to see the confusion and worry that must be only too apparent on her face. But his grip was strong and reassuring and he would not let her go.

Slowly, he nodded. 'I think I can see that now. Can you tell me what's really going on, Kate?'

The concern in his brown eyes, the compassion in his voice, made her long to confide in him, though she scarcely knew him. She couldn't lie to *herself* any longer that there was nothing wrong, so why should she lie to *him?*

She took a deep, steadying breath. 'I've been sitting here for I don't know how long, wondering what the heck has happened to me.'

'You mean, the way you're too frightened to go to Sydney?'

'Is the…the fear that obvious?' So much for her 'nothing bothers me' facade.

'Not immediately. But as I get to know you, I realise—'

'How constricted my life has become?'

'The way you don't seem to want to leave Dolphin Bay.'

She took in a deep intake of breath and let it out as a heavy sigh. 'As I sat here, I came to terms with how my life has become narrower and narrower in its focus. The truly frightening thing is that I realised I hadn't left Dolphin Bay for more than two years.'

He frowned. 'What do you mean?'

She disengaged her hands from his, turned to take a step away so she could think how to explain without him thinking she was a total nut job, then turned back to face him. There was no other way than to state the facts.

'Not just to go to Sydney but to go anywhere outside the town limits. I haven't been to any of the places I used to enjoy. Every time someone wanted me to go to Bateman's Bay for dinner, or to Mogo Zoo to see the white lion cubs, I'd find some excuse. I never made any conscious decision not to leave, it just *happened*.'

'Have you thought about why?'

She could see he was carefully considering his words. Something twisted painfully inside her. Did he think she was crazy? *Maybe she was…*

'I was beginning to suspect I might have some kind of…of agoraphobia. I…I looked it up at one stage. But I don't have full-blown panic attacks, or need someone with me just to go out of the house. I feel absolutely fine until I think about leaving Dolphin Bay.'

'It's not a good idea to label what you're feeling from looking it up the Internet,' he said, more sternly than she had ever heard him speak.

She managed a broken laugh. 'You're right, of course. Self-diagnosis is kinda dumb. But one thing that did give me a light-bulb moment was that agoraphobia—even in its mildest forms—can have had some kind of triggering event.'

'That makes sense. Have you thought back to when your fear started?'

'Yes.'

'Want to tell me about it? I've got broad shoulders.'

She shook her head, unable to speak. Ashamed of how she'd behaved, what she'd become, not so many years ago. 'It's…it's personal. We don't know each other very well.'

'Maybe this is one way to get to know each other better.' That damaged eyebrow gave him a quizzical look. If she ever got the chance, she'd like to ask him how it had happened.

'You might not want to know me better after I've cried all over your shoulder,' she said, trying to turn it into a joke, but her voice betrayed her with a tremor.

'Let me be the judge of that,' he said. 'We've all done things we've regretted, Kate. I certainly have. I reckon whatever it is that's causing your fear could be like a wound that's got infected. You have to lance it to let the poison out or it will continue to fester.'

'Maybe,' she said but didn't sound convinced even to her own ears.

'Look around us,' said Sam, with an all-encompassing wave of his arm. 'There's no one else to hear but me. And I won't be telling anyone.'

She'd held everything inside her so tightly. It might be a relief to let it all out. To Sam. 'Can we sit down? This might take a while.'

'Sure,' he said, casting his gaze around them. 'How about a comfy rock?'

She giggled again, aware of the trill of nervousness that edged it. 'This grassy ledge here might be more comfortable.'

'Much better,' he said, flattening the tall grasses that grew there before he sat down.

She sat down next to him, trying to keep a polite distance, but his shoulders were so broad, his arms so muscular, it was impossible for hers not to nudge them.

'C'mon,' he said. 'Spill.'

She still wasn't at all sure it was a good idea to talk to a man she liked so much about her time with another man. But maybe Sam was right—she needed to release the poison that had been seeping into her soul.

'I…I had a bad experience in Sydney, when I was at university.'

'With a guy?'

She shuddered. 'I can't bear to think about it. I can't even think about his name. In my mind, I only refer to him by his initial.'

Sam tensed. 'Did he… Was it…?'

'No. Not that. I was more than willing to go along with him. That's what makes it so bad, that I could have been so stupid.'

'Or innocent?'

'Maybe that too. I was in my third year of university in Sydney. We met on a vacation ski trip where we were all acting a little wild. He was the handsomest man I'd ever seen.' She snuck a sideways glance at Sam. 'Until now, of course.'

Sam snorted. 'You don't have to say that.'

'But it's true. Seriously.'

'Huh,' he said, but she thought he sounded pleased. 'Go on.'

'I fell for him straight away. Not only was he good-looking, he was funny and kind. Or so I thought.'

'But it was all an act?' Sam's face was grim.

She nodded. 'It was a…a…very physical relationship. I…I hadn't had much experience. He got me well and truly hooked on him and how he could make me feel. I became obsessed with him. It was like…like a drug. Being with him became more important than anything else. I started missing classes, being late with assignments.'

'And then he changed?'

She liked the way he seemed to understand, the way he listened without judging as she finally let it all out. 'It became a…a sexual power game. I wanted love and affection but he wanted something much…much darker than that. He…he had me doing things I'd never dreamed I'd do. Humiliating things. Painful things. But he threatened me that if I didn't go along with what he wanted I'd lose him.'

'And you couldn't bear that,' Sam said slowly.

She looked down at the ground between their bare feet, not wanting to see on his face what he must think of her. 'I thought I loved him. That I couldn't live without him.'

'And you thought he loved you too.'

'That didn't last. He'd been so full-on, but then he became distant. Unavailable. Not answering my calls. But when we saw each other, he'd reassure me nothing was wrong.'

'It was all about control. He wanted to keep you under his thumb.'

She gritted her teeth. No matter what Sam thought about her, she had to tell him the truth. 'I became so anxious that I turned into a person I didn't want to be. I became hysterical if he didn't reply to my texts. Stalked him to see if there was someone else. I dropped out of uni, didn't finish my final semester, just to be at his beck and call. What a fool I was.'

If that wasn't guaranteed to scare Sam off, nothing would be.

He shook his head. 'You were young and vulnerable, he was manipulative.'

'And sadistic,' she said, spitting out the word. 'My suspicions weren't unfounded. I discovered him with another girl. He laughed at my distress.'

'And that was the end?' Sam's voice was gruff.

'He still thought he could pick me up and put me down as he chose. But seeing him with someone else finally knocked some sense into me. To let him get away with that would have been a step too far on a path to self-destruction. I…I walked away.'

'Good for you to find the courage to do that.'

She managed a shaky laugh. 'Oh, I wasn't very courageous. I was scared of how far down I might let myself be dragged. I didn't want to go there.'

'But you did it. You broke the chains. You took the control back.' There was a dark intensity to his eyes as they searched her face.

'Yes. But university was a complete wipe-out. I couldn't stay there to repeat the subjects I'd failed, not when I'd see him around the campus. When the offer came to join the dance troupe, I jumped at it. I got away from Sydney and him and I didn't have to crawl home with my tail between my legs. People thought I'd moved on to something more glamorous and exciting than finishing a business degree. Only I knew what a failure I was.'

He frowned. 'You didn't tell anyone about what had happened?'

'There was a girl at uni who was very supportive. But we lost touch. I didn't really want to be reminded of the person I'd been when I was so obsessed.'

'You didn't tell your mother or your sister?'

'I couldn't bear to tell them I'd failed uni. They thought I'd dropped out because I wanted to dance. They still don't think any different. Still think I threw away my degree.'

'But that meant you didn't ever have to face up to what had happened?'

'That's right. I can't tell you how many times I wished I'd gone home then. Got some help. Because I didn't, it meant I didn't know how to cope with the next situation that made me doubt myself.'

She took a deep breath and edged away from him. 'But I think you've heard enough of my history for one day.'

He put his hand out to draw her back to him but then he hesitated, his dark brows drawn together, and dropped his hand back to his side. She couldn't bear it if he thought she didn't want his touch, his kisses, *him.* She took a step that brought her closer to him, her gaze locked with his. 'Hold me, Sam,' she said. 'Please?'

He put his arm around her shoulder and drew her back closer so her head rested on his shoulder. It was, indeed, broad. And solid, warm and comforting. 'You need to get all that poison out. If there's more, I want to hear it,' he said.

CHAPTER NINE

SAM HAD ALWAYS scorned the concept of love at first sight. In his book, instant attraction was all about sex, not love. The proof had been his parents' disastrous 'marry in haste, repent at leisure' marriage. And yet, although he wanted to kiss her, hold her, make love to her, he felt more than physical attraction for Kate—something that had been there from the first time they'd met. A feeling that was so strong, it made any further pretence at a business-only relationship seem farcical.

He was surprised and pleased, after the way she had pushed him away from their kiss the previous day, that she had actually sought his touch. He held her close to him, her bright head nestled on his shoulder, the folds of her blue dress brushing his legs, her hand resting lightly on his knee. He breathed in her heady, already so familiar scent. And he didn't want to let her go.

But this was no simple boy-meets-girl scenario.

Beneath that open, vivacious exterior Kate seemed to be a seething mass of insecurities, far from the straightforward person he'd thought she was. She'd been hiding secrets for years. Were there more? Could he deal with them?

With every fibre of his being he wanted to help her. But he didn't know how he could, other than being supportive. Nothing in his life experience had prepared him for this.

She shifted back from him, not so that she eluded the protective curve of his arm but so he could see her face.

'Can I tell you how good it is to talk to you like this?' she said.

Shadows from the overhanging trees flickered across her face. It made it difficult to read her eyes.

'If it helps, I'm glad.' He wasn't sure what else he could say. He risked dropping a kiss on her bare, smooth shoulder. She didn't flinch from him—that was progress.

'Are you sure you want to hear more? The second incident wasn't such a big deal. Not nearly as traumatic. I mightn't even mention it if I wasn't trying to find what triggered my aversion to leaving the city limits.'

'Bring it on. Did something happen while you were on tour with the dance troupe?'

Her hair was pulled back in a tie and he could see every nuance of her expression. She pulled a puzzled 'Kate' face. 'How did you know that?'

'Lucky guess,' he said, not adding that as soon as she'd started to talk about it her stilted words had become a dead giveaway.

'The injured ankle wasn't how my career as a cabaret dancer ended,' she said. 'Though I did hurt my ankle in a triple pirouette that collapsed in a less-than-graceful stumble.'

After the story of her abuse at the hands of her university lover, he wasn't at all certain he wanted to hear this double whammy, but he asked anyway. 'So how did it end?'

'After the injury healed, I joined the troupe again. They were about to go to Spain. I was so looking forward to it.'

'You would have gone overseas?' He couldn't keep the surprise from his voice.

'Yes. That's the crazy thing. I was so looking forward to it. Not a trace of this…this current affliction. We'd done a few weeks in New Zealand and I'd loved it. I'd even bought myself a "teach yourself Spanish" CD.'

The best thing, he figured, was to let her talk. 'So what happened to change things?'

'We had an extended stay at a club in a big country town in western New South Wales. There was a guy.' She rolled her eyes. 'Yeah, I know—another guy.'

'I should imagine there were a lot of guys interested in you,' he said drily. Smart. Beautiful. A dancer. She must have been besieged.

'Maybe,' she said with a wobbly smile. 'But I wasn't interested in *them*. In fact, after my experience at uni I'd sworn off men. I…didn't feel I could trust anyone.'

'Understandable,' he said, while thinking of a few choice words to describe the creep who had treated a vulnerable girl with such contempt and cruelty.

'There were often men at the stage door hoping to meet the dancers but I never took any notice of them. This guy seemed different. A gentleman. The Aussie grazier with the Akubra hat, the tweed jacket, the moleskin jeans. Older than the guys I'd dated. We had a drink after the show one evening and he was charming. He bred horses on his property and showed me photos. His historic old homestead, quite a distance out of town, looked amazing. And there were photos of foals. He asked me would I like to come and see the foals.'

'And of course you said yes.'

'Who could resist foals? They looked adorable with their long, baby legs. I couldn't wait to pet them.'

'You let down your guard.'

'He…he seemed so nice…'

'I can hear an "until" in your voice.'

Kate reached down to pick up a fallen eucalypt leaf. She started to tear it into tiny strips, releasing the sharp tang of eucalyptus oil to mingle with the salt of the breeze that wafted over them. 'Until he tried to kiss me and wouldn't take no for an answer. He wanted more than kisses. Got angry when I refused. Told me I was asking for it by dressing in sexy costumes and dancing provocatively onstage.'

Sam surprised himself with the growl of anger that rumbled from his throat and the string of swear words directed at her attacker.

'I used some of those words, too,' she said. 'But I got away, thank heaven. Luckily some sense of caution had made me refuse his offer of a ride to his place. I'd borrowed a car to get out there, so was able to get back under my own steam. The troupe left town the next day. I've never been so glad to get out of a place.'

'Did you report him?'

She shook her head. 'I was strong and agile and very angry—he didn't get anywhere near me.'

'You were lucky.' If he could get his hands on him, the guy would know not to go anywhere near her again.

'I know. I shook for hours when I got back when I thought about how differently it might have ended. He… he'd backed me into a boot room and closed the door.'

'That's why you reacted the way you did in the shed yesterday?'

Mutely, she nodded.

'Please tell me you confided in someone about the attack.'

'I didn't tell anyone. It made me look so stupid. The more experienced girls would never have gone off alone with a stage-door stalker.'

'He was cunning to use baby horses as a lure.'

'I know, which made me look even stupider for falling for it. And again, I began to doubt myself.'

'What do you mean?'

She got up from the ledge, threw the shredded leaf to the ground. 'The farmer guy was right in a way. Our dance costumes *were* form-fitting. Modern dance moves *can* be provocative. For one of our routines we had to dress as white poodles and bark as we danced. Can you imagine?'

She seemed determined to put a light spin to her story. She even took a few graceful, prancing steps on the sandy ground, mimed a dog's paws held out in front of her, her head alert to one side.

'You had to bark like a dog?' It took an effort not to laugh.

'Not just any old dog. A poodle. I listened to how a poodle barked in the interests of authenticity.' She paused. 'Go on—you're allowed to laugh. I get quite hysterical when I remember it. You'd be hysterical too if you saw us in those skin-tight white costumes with pompom poodle-tails on our butts and fluffy poodle ears on our heads.'

'I don't actually think I'd be laughing. It sounds very cute to me.' And very sexy. It wasn't difficult to see how a guy in the audience had got obsessed with her.

'There was a circus ringmaster cracking his whip as we danced and barked, which was kinda weird.'

This time he couldn't stop the laugh. 'I'm sure you made a gorgeous poodle.'

She pulled another of those cute Kate faces. 'You never know, I might do my poodle bark for you some time. I got quite good at it.'

He could only imagine. 'I'd like to see you dance.'

'Wearing a poodle costume?'

'Maybe. Or a white dress, like in that photo in your living room.'

This time the face she pulled was wistful, her eyes shadowed with regret. 'We danced *Swan Lake* that year for the end-of-year concert. I was Odette.'

'How fortunate that *Swan Lake* is the only ballet I've ever seen. So I actually know what you're talking about.'

'You won't see me perform it again. I stopped dancing soon after that near escape, even social dancing. The farmer guy's words kept going around and around in my head. Even though I'd been dancing since I was a child, I suddenly lost it. Became self-conscious, too aware of how I looked. How the men in the audience might perceive me. Scared, I guess.'

'Scared?'

'Scared of the next incident when some weirdo guy might think I was asking for it.' She paused. 'Now you know all my secrets. All my disasters updated.'

Sam jumped up from the ledge and took the few steps needed to reach her. But he didn't hug her close like he wanted to. Not when she'd just been remembering an assault.

'Kate, what that guy did was not your fault. What the guy in Sydney did wasn't your fault.'

Slowly, she nodded. 'I know. But, no matter how many times I told myself that, I didn't quite believe it. Was it something about me that attracted creepy guys? Why didn't I see them for what they were? Whatever; I couldn't get out there onstage and dance any more. I blamed it on my ankle but that didn't fool people for long. When Mum called to say she'd broken her arm and could I come home for a few weeks, I quit the dance company before they had a chance to sack me.'

'And you haven't danced since.'

'Sadly, no. I came back here where I know everyone and they know me. There were no opportunities to dance professionally. I'm qualified to teach dance but I didn't even want to do that.'

'And here you stayed.'

'No one knew what had happened to me—the abusive boyfriend; the scary experience with the farmer guy. Mum and Emily were glad to see me back. I was wanted, I was needed, and I just settled back into life here.'

'You didn't talk to anyone when you got back? Your family doctor, maybe?'

She shrugged. 'There was nothing to talk about. I blamed everything that happened on being away from home. Once I was home, it was okay.

'So you pretended it hadn't happened.'

'That's right. I felt safe here. Unthreatened.'

'I told you, small-town life is not for me. But, after dinner at your place last night, I can see the attraction for you. Your mum is such a nice lady—not to mention an incredible cook. And Emily is delightful. If I had a family like yours, I'd be tempted to stay here for ever too.'

But Kate was of an age when she should be making her own home. Thinking about starting her own family. *So should he.*

He realised with a sudden flash of clarity that the reason he spent so much time in the workplace was that it had become a substitute for family. At work he got recognition, admiration, companionship, security.

'Your family isn't like that?' she said, frowning.

'My family was so far removed from yours, there isn't any comparison. Home was like a battlefield where both sides have made a truce but occasionally resume hostilities. My mother was my father's second wife. He was still grieving his first wife when he met Vivien and—'

Kate put up her hand to interrupt him. 'Who is Vivien?'

'My mother. She doesn't like be called Mum or Mother—says it makes her feel too old.' He hated explaining it, as he'd always hated explaining it. Sitting in Kate's house, with her mother fussing over him with tea and home-baked cake, he had felt a tug of envy. His mother had not been the cake-baking, cosy type.

For once, Kate seemed lost for words. 'That's, uh, unusual. Even when you were a little boy?'

'Even when I was so little I had trouble pronouncing "Vivien".' He made a joke of it, but he'd never liked calling his mother by her name. If she hadn't wanted to be thought of as a mother, what had that meant to his identity as a son?

'You poor little thing,' said Kate. 'I mean you *were* a poor little thing. I don't mean you're a poor little thing *now*. In fact, you're rather big and—'

'I get it,' he said with a laugh.

Kate was back in full stickybeak mode but he had the distinct impression she was using it to distract him. 'You have to tell me more. We should shut up about me now. I still have one more question to go, you know; I've been saving it to find out about—'

He cut across her. 'We can talk about me later. Right now, we need to concentrate on you.'

She fell silent. 'Try to sort me out, you mean?' Her mouth turned downward so far it was almost comical.

'Don't be so hard on yourself. You were young, you had some traumatic experiences. You retreated to the safe place you needed to get over them.' She started to wring her hands together, something he noticed she did when she was upset.

'That safe place seems to have become a comfortable prison,' she muttered.

Without a word, he reached out and stilled her hands with his. 'That you now realise you have to release yourself from.'

He didn't know where these words of comfort came from other than a deep need to connect with her—maybe from his management training. It certainly didn't come from the tough love dished out by his parents. But it seemed to be helping Kate and that was all that counted.

She sighed. 'I'm angry at myself that I took the comfortable option instead of confronting my problems. Problems that, as you said, must have festered away.'

'Don't beat yourself up about it. Sounds like you've had a good life in Dolphin Bay.' He looked around him. 'Idyllic' really was the right word to describe their surroundings. 'There are worse places to be holed up while you heal.'

She slammed one fist into another. 'But it's not enough any more. I feel like I'm in a science fiction story where some big, transparent dome is over the town that only I'm aware of and I can't get past it. Meeting you has reminded me of what I'm missing out on.'

'True. For one thing, there's a whole, wide world of fabulous hotels out there for you to explore.' He kept his tone light, teasing, to defuse the anger she was turning on herself.

'You're right,' she said, after a long pause. 'Starting with that fabulous palace hotel in India. I looked it up after you told me about it. I so want to see it for myself.'

'I studied engineering at university, not psychology. But that seems to make sense. To go see a maharajah's palace is as good an incentive as any for you to break out.'

'I'm going to aim for it—something to focus on.' She looked up at him, her face still and very serious. Then she reached up and touched his cheek with her cool, eucalyptus-scented fingers. 'Sam, thank you for being the first person I've ever told anything about all this.'

Knowing he had helped her felt good. He caught her hand with his. 'Don't let me be the last. Talk to your mother. Perhaps even seek professional help,' he said. 'We really don't want you trapped inside that dome.'

'But only *I* can get over it. No one can do that for me.' She kept hold of his hand as she spoke.

'You've taken the first step by realising you need help,' he said.

Her eyes widened. 'Sam Lancaster, how did you get to be so wise?'

'I'm not wise. I…I just like you.' Maybe that was all it took—to care enough about another person to help her. It might transcend everything.

'I'm glad to hear that. Because…because I like you too,' she said.

Her eyes were in shadow but amazingly green, the pupils very large as she looked back at him. Again, there was that long moment of silent communication between them. She swayed towards him. Before he could think any further about it, he caught her and lowered his head to kiss her, first on each of those delightful dimples, then her pretty mouth. But this time, now he understood where she was coming from, he held back so the kiss stayed tender and non-threatening.

She gave a gasp of surprise followed by a murmur of pleasure as she relaxed into the kiss. Her arms slid up around his neck and she pulled his head closer. The kiss started as a light brushing of lips, returned tentatively at first as if she were wary, then more passionately, perhaps as she realised she was safe with him. Her warm lips, the cool taste of her tongue, ignited his hunger for her. A shudder of want ran through him as he deepened the kiss. But as it became more urgent she broke away, gasping, her face flushed.

'Sam. Wow. That…that was wonderful. Yesterday was wonderful. And…and I wasn't scared.'

'You will *never* have cause to be frightened of me,' he said.

He would do all he could to make sure she trusted him. But the confusion and doubt on her face made him realise it would not be plain sailing.

'Thank you,' she said and squeezed his hand. 'But I…I don't know that I'm ready for…for more yet. I…I haven't got anything to give you when I'm such a mess.'

He had trouble keeping his voice even, still reeling from the impact of her kiss. From knowing he wanted so much more. 'You're not a mess. You're a smart, special woman who just has the one problem to deal with.' He dropped a light kiss on her cheek. 'And I've got the takeover bid for the business looming.'

He should take his cue from her—the last thing he needed right now was the complication of a relationship. Not when he only had a few days to make a decision that would impact on so many other people.

Though wasn't he doing what he always did—using work as an excuse for keeping his distance?

'I guess we both have issues to deal with,' she said. She looked up at him. 'Sam, you've been such a help to me today, I'd love to be able to help you. If you want someone to talk over your business stuff with, well, I'm your girl. Not that I know anything about construction, but I could be a sounding board.'

'Thanks,' he said. He was touched by her offer, but the decision whether or not to sell the company his grandfather, his father and then he himself had invested their lives in rested firmly on his own shoulders.

She made a game of fanning herself with one graceful, elegant hand. 'I'm going to dip my feet in the water to cool off. Want to come with me?'

She walked into the ankle-deep shallows at the river's edge and he fell into step beside her.

Cooling off seemed like a very good idea.

* * *

Sam had kissed her again and Kate had loved every moment of it. There'd been no panic, no fear, just pleasure, comfort and excitement. But now wasn't the time for further kissing—though there was nothing she'd rather be doing. She knew, deep down, that until she sorted out her agoraphobia—if that was what it was—kissing Sam would only complicate things.

When she'd first seen him, her instincts had told her he was dangerous. Now she was convinced he wasn't dangerous in the way she had feared. The real danger was to her heart.

It would be only too easy to fall in love with Sam.

And she couldn't handle that right now.

To talk about all that stuff she'd kept bottled up inside her for so long had been truly liberating. Sam was a wonderful listener and seemed to have an instinct for drawing out her most painful memories. What she'd liked most was that he had given her good advice without judging her.

'When did you realise that Dolphin Bay had become a prison?' he said now as they walked hand in hand in the ankle-deep water at the edge of the lagoon.

'Only recently. The wedding has brought it all into focus. And…and it's only today, here by myself in this place that I love, that I realised how restricted my life had become. That…that it isn't enough any more.'

'You might have to dig down deeper under the scars from the past to find out how to fix it,' he said, obviously choosing his words carefully.

She turned away. 'You must think I'm a neurotic wreck.' She tried to make a joke of it, but her words came out as sounding anything but funny. With a tug to her hand, he pulled her back to face him.

'Of course I don't think you're a neurotic wreck. In fact, I don't know how you've held it together this long.'

'Obviously I didn't hold it together. I'm a recluse.'

'Where do you get these labels from? You're far from being a recluse. You have family and friends who all care for you.'

'I haven't dated for years, you know.'

'That I find very difficult to believe.' The admiration in his eyes took the sting out of her admission.

'I didn't trust my judgement. I couldn't tell the bad guys from the good guys.'

'Have you made a judgement of me?'

'You're…you're definitely one of the good guys.' Of her intuition, she was absolutely certain.

'Good,' he said. 'So where did Jesse fit in?'

'I've been thinking about that too. Trying to analyse how I got it so wrong.'

'Seems to me you got attached to Jesse about the same time as your dad moved out.'

She thought back to that traumatic time. 'Maybe. Everything else got turned upside down but my friend was still there. Stable. Secure. Maybe I got to believe all those family jokes about if we didn't each meet someone else we'd end up together.'

'Maybe that stopped you from getting serious about someone else.'

'You mean, after I came back here I used a crush on Jesse to protect myself from taking risks with other guys?'

'Could be.'

'It…it makes a strange kind of sense,' she said slowly.

Sam glanced down at his watch. 'Talking of Jesse, Ben and Sandy—if we leave now we can meet our friends in Sydney in time for dinner. What do you think?'

She swallowed hard at the sudden constriction in her

throat. 'I want to go. I really do. I feel sick that I've let them down—feel even sicker that I've let myself down with this stupid fear.' She forced bravado into her voice. 'Maybe…maybe I'm ready to try again. With you to hold my hand, that is.'

'I can drive us. But are you sure you want to go?'

She wasn't at all sure. But she was determined to give it a try. For Sandy. For Ben. For Sam, who'd been so patient with her.

She held on to his hand as they made their way back via the quicker route up through the bushland and along the pathways that led past the site for the new hotel. But, as they got closer to the town centre where she'd parked her car, Kate dropped his hand.

'I know it's ironic, as I'm the biggest gossip in town myself, but I've had enough of people talking about me,' she explained. 'I want to keep our…our friendship to ourselves.'

'Fair enough. I don't like people talking about my business either.' He stopped. 'But I do like holding your hand,' he said with a grin that warmed her heart.

Kate was okay getting into her car and driving home with Sam seated next to her. She was okay packing an overnight bag while Sam checked on his carpentry work out in the shed. She only started to get shaky as she drove back to the hotel to transfer to Sam's sports car.

'You okay?' he asked.

'Yep,' she said, pasting on that cheerful smile, hoping it would give her the courage and strength she so severely lacked.

But as soon as Sam opened the passenger door for her to get in she was again gripped by fear. As she went to slide into the seat, her knees went to jelly. Nausea rose in her throat and she started to shake.

She gasped for air. 'I can't do it, Sam. I thought I could, but I can't.'

He pulled her out of the car and held her to him, patting her on the back, making soothing, wordless sounds until the shaking stopped. She relaxed against him, beyond caring who saw her or what they might say.

'Too much, too soon,' he said.

She pulled away. 'Maybe,' she said. 'But I'm so angry with myself, so disappointed…'

'So we don't go to Sydney. What's the fuss?'

'You could still go. You've got plenty of time to get up there.'

'What's the point of a groomsman going out on the town without his bridesmaid?'

'You can still have fun in Sydney. Lizzie booked a really nice venue.'

'No arguments. I can go out in Sydney any time. I'm staying here with you.'

'But—'

He placed his index finger over her lips. 'No buts. We're going to look at this afternoon like it's a bonus. It gives us more time to spend working on the arch.'

She took a few more deep breaths, felt her heart rate returning to normal.

'I haven't shown you yet how good I am as a handy-woman.'

'Now's your chance,' he said. 'Then we're going to go on that date.'

'Wh-what about your no dating rule?'

'I own the company; I make the rules. I say to hell with that rule—as least, as it applies to you. I'm taking you out to dinner. We'll have our own party.'

She laughed with relief and a bubbling excitement. 'As Ben so obviously tried to set me up with you, I don't think there's a "no dating Sam" rule in place. It was more my own…my own fears giving me an excuse.'

'Let's book the best restaurant in Dolphin Bay.'

'The Harbourside is the best restaurant,' she said loyally.

'Okay—the second-best restaurant in Dolphin Bay,' he said. 'Or Thai take-out on the pier. Or fish and chips at the pub. Your choice.'

She smiled, relieved she could feel normal again, excited at the thought of dinner with Sam. 'I'm overwhelmed by the responsibility of the decision. But Thai does sound kind of tempting.'

'Thai it is—and lots of it. I'm starving.'

'Are you always hungry?'

'Always,' he said.

She laughed. 'I'm really getting to know you, aren't I?'

While she kept a happy smile pasted to her face, inside Kate wasn't so happy. The more she got to know Sam, the more she liked him.

But what future could there be for a man who travelled the world and a girl who was too scared to go further than the outskirts of her home town?

CHAPTER TEN

SANDY HAD BEEN RIGHT, Kate realised on the day of the wedding. A wedding *was* more fun for a bridesmaid when she had a handsome groomsman in tow. It was also more fun for a wedding planner when that groomsman had volunteered to be her helper—not only with the construction of the bridal arch, but also with other last-minute jobs along the way.

Not that Sam and she had spent much time together since their Thai take-out dinner. She'd still had her shifts at the hotel. And Sam had seemed to be in one conference call or video call after another. So much for that break from his business.

But, despite his grumbling about waste-of-time wedding fripperies, Sam had not only finished the arch but had also helped Sandy and her with writing the place cards and Emily with counting out the sugared almonds to put in the tulle-wrapped wedding favours. He had, however, point-blank refused to tie pretty pastel ribbons on them.

Now Ben and Sandy's big day was here. Dolphin Bay had, thank heaven, put on its finest weather for the last weekend of daylight saving time—although Kate didn't take the good weather for granted. With a ceremony being held outdoors on the beach, she'd planned alternative arrangements to cover all contingencies, from heatwave to hailstorm.

At noon she was still in the function room at the Hotel Harbourside, where the reception was to be held, making final checks on the arrangements for the buffet-style meal.

Sliding doors opened out onto an ocean-facing balcony that gave a good view of the ceremony site on the beach below. Every few minutes she dashed out to see if the sky was indeed still perfectly blue and free of clouds, the wind still the gentle zephyr that would not make an organza-adorned arch suddenly become airborne as the bride and groom exchanged their vows. Not unnecessary anxiety, she told herself, for a wedding scheduled to start in just four hours.

Everything that could be checked off on her multiple pages of lists had been checked off. Everyone who had needed to be briefed on their wedding duties had been briefed. Now it was time for the hotel staff to take over. And for her to start having fun.

But, as she headed for the door that led into the hotel corridor, she couldn't resist turning back and picking up a silver serving platter to see if it had been polished as directed. She peered closely at it, fearing she saw a scratch.

'Ready to stop being an obsessive wedding planner and start being a bridesmaid? I've been dispatched to find you.' Sam's deep, resonant voice coming from behind her made her jump so she nearly dropped the platter. She hadn't heard him come in.

She turned to face him and halted halfway. Her heart seemed to stop as it always did at the first sight of this man who took up so much space in her thoughts. He'd shaved and had had his hair cut. She smiled. 'You look different,' she said, after a long moment when her heartbeat had returned somewhat to normal. 'Just as handsome, but different.'

And even hotter than when she'd last seen him.

'I'm taking my groomsman duties seriously,' Sam said. 'Ben wanted me clean shaven, so I got clean shaven.'

She was unable to resist reaching up and tracing the smooth line of his jaw with her fingers. She would have liked to kiss him, but two of the waiting staff were polishing champagne flutes at the other end of the room. 'You look more corporate than carpenter and that takes a little getting used to. But I like it. And the haircut. Though, I have to say, I really liked the stubble.'

'I guarantee that'll be back by morning,' he said with a grin.

"Good," she said.

She put her hand on his arm. 'Are you okay with all this wedding stuff? I mean, it isn't weird for you when your own wedding was cancelled? I hate to think it might bring back sad memories.'

'I'm good with it. I wasn't actually there for all my own wedding preparations. I was working in Queensland or Western Australia, or Singapore or somewhere else far away.'

'Your fiancée mustn't have been too happy about that.'

'She wasn't. To the point she accused me of being so uninvolved with the preparations, she didn't think I was interested in the wedding or, ultimately, truly interested in her.'

Kate didn't know what she could say to that other than a polite murmur. 'I see.'

'Her tipping point was when I couldn't make the rehearsal because it clashed with an important business engagement.'

Suddenly Kate felt more than a touch of sympathy for

Sam's unknown fiancée. 'I would have been furious if I were her.'

'She was. That's when she threw her engagement ring at me and told me the wedding was off.'

'And you were surprised?'

'Well, yes.'

'Now that you've had time to reflect about it, are you still surprised?'

He grinned. 'No.'

'Good. I would have had to revise my opinion of you if you had said yes.'

'I've had plenty of time to reflect that I was a selfish workaholic, too obsessed with proving myself to my father to be a good boyfriend or a good fiancé. Certainly, I wouldn't have been a good husband.'

'So you weren't really ready to get married?'

'Probably not. But I've also had time to think about whether Frances was right. Maybe…maybe I just didn't love her enough to make that level of commitment and subconsciously used work as an excuse.' He paused and she could see remembered pain in his eyes. 'I was gutted at the time, though. We'd been together for years.'

'Would you say you're still a selfish workaholic?' Kate asked, unable to stop a twinge of jealousy at the thought of the woman who'd shared Sam's life for so long.

'Probably. That's one reason I'm considering selling the company. I suspect I've given too much of my life to it—given it too much importance at the cost of other more important things.'

Kate was just about to reply when a tall, slender girl with a mop of silvery blonde curls poked her head around the door. 'There you are, Kate. The hairdresser, make-up artist and manicurist are all waiting for us.' Lizzie scowled at Sam. 'You, Sam, were charged with getting Kate up to

Sandy's suite,' she scolded. 'We've got secret bridesmaids' business to attend to.'

Kate put up her hand. 'Just one more minute, Lizzie,' she said.

Lizzie folded her arms in front of her chest and ostentatiously tapped her foot. 'I'm going to wait right here to make sure you don't disappear.'

Kate leaned up to whisper in Sam's ear. 'Is everything okay with the arch?'

'Yes,' he murmured. 'Your mother and a friend from the hospital—some guy named Colin—are going to drive the van down to the beach. I'll slip out at the time we arranged and they'll help me install it.'

'Fantastic. Thank you,' she whispered. 'I can't wait to see it.'

'Hurry up, Kate,' urged Lizzie.

'Okay, okay,' said Kate and fled the room.

Sam hadn't been one hundred per cent honest with Kate. The frenzied wedding activities *had* brought back memories of his own abruptly terminated nuptials nearly two years ago.

Seeing at close quarters the levels of planning that went into even a simple ceremony like Ben and Sandy's made him realise how badly he'd neglected Frances in the months leading up to their big, showy wedding. On many of the times she'd asked for a decision, he'd brushed her aside with his stock replies: 'You decide,' or 'I'll leave it to you.' He hadn't cooperated with his mother, either, who had thrown herself into the elaborate preparations with great gusto. With hindsight, he realised his mother had done a lot to help Frances when it should have been *him* doing the helping.

Thinking about how he'd behaved made him feel

vaguely ashamed. At the time, he had paid lip service to an apology. But, feeling aggrieved, he hadn't really been sure what he had done to deserve the cancellation of his wedding and the dumping by his fiancée.

Being around Kate, her family and friends made him realise exactly what he'd done wrong. And that he'd be damned sure he got it right the next time round.

Being around Kate was also making him question how he'd felt about his former fiancée. After several years together, he had never felt for Frances what he already felt for Kate. If he were about to marry Kate—and of course that was purely a hypothetical situation—no way would he be away in another country. He would want to be with his bride-to-be every minute, working alongside her to plan their future together. *Hypothetically, of course.*

Now he stood barefoot on the sand, lined up with Ben and Jesse under the arch he had built with Kate in her father's shed. It held firm in the breeze coming off the waters of the bay. Ben, in that jesting way of good mates, had told him that he had a bright future ahead of him making gimcracks for weddings. Because it was Ben's day, he had let him get away with it.

The three men waited for the bridesmaids and then the bride to walk down the sandy aisle that had been formed between rows of folding white chairs and delineated with two rows of sea shells.

Suddenly the guests swivelled around to a collective sigh. 'Oohs' and 'aahs' greeted the sight of Lizzie's five-year-old daughter, Amy. But, by the time Amy was half-way down the aisle, Sam only had eyes for the beautiful red-haired bridesmaid who followed her.

He'd never understood the expression 'took his breath away' until now. In bare feet, Kate moved like the dancer she was, seeming to glide along the sand towards him.

Her strapless peach dress showed off her graceful shoulders and arms, and clung to her curves before it ended just below her knees. Her hair, pulled up off her face with some of it tumbling down her shoulders, shone like a halo in the afternoon sun.

Her glorious smile captivated him as it had the first time he'd seen her. Only this time her smile seemed only for him. Somehow, with just a glance, she seemed to convey how happy she was to be sharing this day with him. He smiled back, unable to take his eyes off her. When she reached the arch, he stepped forward to offer her his arm to guide her to the bride's side of the area. He had to resist a strong impulse to gather her to him and keep her by his side, an arm planted possessively around her waist.

Kate couldn't help a moment of self-congratulation at how well the shades of the sunset colour-scheme worked. She herself wore apricot, Lizzie a shade that veered towards tangerine and little Amy's white dress had a big bow in a pale tint of magenta. The three men were handsome in chinos and loose white shirts. But Sam was the one who made her heart race, who made her aware of where he was at all times without her even having to look.

She kept sneaking sideways glimpses at him, glances that were often intercepted and ended in secret smiles. Every minute she knew him, he seemed to grow more attractive. Not just in his looks but also in his personality, which was funnier, kinder and more thoughtful than she could have imagined—though she didn't let herself forget there must be a ruthless side to him too.

For a moment, when he had stepped forward to take her arm, she had indulged in a fantasy of what it might be like if she'd been walking up an aisle to meet him as her groom. She had immediately dismissed the thought as impossible but its warmth lingered in her mind. How was she going to endure it when he went back to Sydney the next day?

She forced her gaze away from Sam and straight ahead to where Sandy was about to commence her walk down the aisle.

But first it was Hobo's turn. Ben's mother Maura—officially appointed by Kate as dog-handler—had spent days training Hobo to sedately stroll down the aisle and take his place with Ben under the arch. The big, shaggy golden retriever—wearing a white ribbon around his neck, slightly chewed around the ends—started off fine, sitting as directed at the head of the aisle, giving the guests a big, doggy smile. There was a furious clicking of cameras.

'Good boy, Hobo,' Kate heard Maura whisper. But her praise was premature. Hobo caught sight of Ben, lolloped off down the aisle and came to a skidding halt next to his master's feet, spraying sand around him as he landed.

The guests erupted into laughter and Sandy was laughing too as she started her walk down the aisle. It was a perfect start to the ceremony, Kate thought, the laughter vanquishing any last-minute nerves or tension.

When Ben and Sandy exchanged their vows in front of the celebrant, there wasn't a sound except their murmured 'I do'—and the occasional muffled sob and sniffle from the guests.

As she watched them, Kate was tearing up too. She couldn't help an ache in her heart—not from envy of the bride and groom but a longing for the same kind of happiness for herself one day. She'd never really let herself imagine being married, having children, but of course she wanted all that one day.

She just had to get the man right.

She stole another surreptitious glance at Sam, to find

him looking to her too. Did she imagine a hint of the same longing in his eyes? *If only...*

Weddings seemed to dredge up so many deeply submerged emotions and bring them to the surface. She had to be careful she didn't let her imagination run riot and believe Sam felt in any way the same as she did.

But, when the newlyweds moved off to the small table they had set up for the signing of the official papers, Sam was next to her the first second he could be. He interlinked his fingers with hers and drew her to him for a swift, sweet kiss. 'You outshone the bride,' he murmured.

She protested, of course, but was deeply, secretly pleased. She wondered if anyone had noticed their kiss but decided she didn't care. Forget the 'poor Kate' whispers. She reckoned there was more likely to be whispers of 'lucky Kate'.

She *was* lucky to have met him. And, if tonight was the only time she ever had with Sam, she was going to darn well enjoy every minute of it.

CHAPTER ELEVEN

SAM FELT A certain envy at the newlyweds' obvious joy in each other. Being part of the wedding ceremony had stirred emotions in him he'd had no idea existed. Above all, it had forced him to face up to what he could not continue to deny to himself: he was besotted with Kate. No matter how much he fought the concept, he had fallen fast and hard for her.

From his seat at the bride and groom's table he watched Kate as she flitted her way around the wedding reception like a bright flame; her hair, her dress, her smile made her easy to pick out in the crowd.

'She's a great girl, isn't she?' said Lizzie, who was sitting next to him. Was it so obvious that he couldn't keep his eyes off Kate?

'Yup,' he said, not wanting to be distracted.

Lizzie laughed. 'Don't worry, your secret is safe with me.'

He twisted to face her. 'What do you mean?'

'That you're smitten with Kate.' He started to protest but she spoke over him. 'Don't worry. I don't think too many other people have noticed. They're all still determined to pair her off with the home-town favourite, Jesse Morgan. I don't know how Kate feels about that. I thought that might have been the reason why she didn't come up to Sydney on Wednesday.'

A tightness in her voice made Sam look more closely at Lizzie. 'Kate likes him as a friend, almost a brother, that's all.' He was surprised by the flash of relief that flickered across Lizzie's face. 'But you—you like Jesse?'

She flushed. 'Of course I don't. He's arrogant. A player. Much too handsome for his own good and way too sure of himself.'

Sam stored her excessive denial away to share with Kate later. In the meantime, he had to stick up for his friend. 'Actually, Jesse is a mate of mine and a really good guy. He's confident, not arrogant. And he's not a player.'

Lizzie snorted. 'I'll have to take your word for it.'

Lizzie had an acerbic edge to her and possibly too many glasses of champagne on board. Sam decided he didn't want to engage in any further discussion about Jesse. He was relieved when she excused herself to go and have a word with her sister.

He drummed his fingers on the tabletop and wished Kate would come back to her chair. Ideally, he wanted her to be by his side all evening, but that wasn't going to happen—not with the number of people who were waylaying her for a chat. She knew everyone and they knew her. No wonder she had found it so easy to stay in this town for so long; there was no denying the sense of community.

But could he live here?

Despite his aversion to small-town life, it was a question he had to ask himself. What if Kate was unable to get over her problem, to get out from under that invisible dome? The way he felt about her, he would find it untenable for them not to be in the same town if anything developed between them. If she couldn't come to him in Sydney, might he have to come to her in Dolphin Bay?

If it meant being with Kate, he had to consider it.

When his father had had one too many drinks, he'd

sometimes decided to give his son advice on women. It had always been the same—telling Sam to be sure he knew a woman really well before he considered commitment. The old 'marry in haste, repent at leisure' thing would inevitably come up. His dad had adored his first wife, the only blight on the marriage being the fact they hadn't had children. He had been devastated when she'd died, had not been able to handle being on his own. Quite soon after, he'd met Vivien and had married her within months. By the time they'd realised it was a mistake, Sam had been on the way. They'd never actually said so, but he'd come to believe his parents had only stayed together for their child's sake.

Sam wasn't ready to propose to Kate after only a week. That would be crazy. But he didn't want to wait for ever to have her beside him, sharing his life.

He wanted what Ben and Sandy had, and he wanted it with Kate.

Kate slid into the chair beside him and hooked her arm through his. 'My mouth is aching from smiling so much and I'm not even the bride,' she said. 'Are you having fun?'

'Now you're back with me, the fun is back on track,' he said.

'The perfect reply,' she said, with the full-on dimpled smile that was getting such a workout. This was the vivacious, bubbly Kate everyone knew. Looking at her flushed, happy face, it was difficult to believe she had secrets that haunted her.

'You must be pleased at how well everything is going,' he said. 'Congratulations to the wedding planner.'

'Congratulations to the world's best wedding-arch builder,' she said. 'It was a big hit.'

'I'm glad we made the effort.' He realised he had fallen into talking about 'we'—and he liked the feeling.

'Clever us.' She sighed. 'I can't believe how fast it's gone. All that work and it's over in a matter of hours. But now the speeches are done, the band is starting up and we can all relax.'

On cue, the band started to play and the MC announced it was time for the bride and groom to dance the first dance to a medley of popular love songs.

Sam noticed Kate go so pale, her freckles stood out. She looked anything but relaxed. 'Are you okay?'

He noticed she was wringing her hands together under the table. 'I didn't think this through,' she said in an undertone. 'According to the order of the reception, the best man and chief bridesmaid will get up to dance next. Then they'll expect you and me to get up.'

'I'm okay with that, if you don't mind my two left feet.'

'It's not that. It's me. I can't dance—I don't dance—especially not in front of all these people.'

Her panicked voice reminded Sam all over again of the way Kate's fears had paralysed her. Lizzie had been correct—he was smitten with Kate. But would he be able to help her overcome those fears so she could move on to a less constricted life? If she couldn't, would there be any chance of a future for them?

He covered her hands with his much bigger ones to soothe their anxious twisting. 'No one is going to force you. But I do think, as you've been such an important part of this wedding, you're expected to get up on the dance floor. I'll lead you on and we can shuffle.'

'Shuffle?'

'Stand there and sway to the music. That way you don't have to dance, I don't have to dance—and you won't let your friends down.'

She took a deep breath and Sam could see what an effort it was for her. 'All those years of dance training and it comes to this,' she said with that bitter twist to her mouth.

'You're in a room full of friends,' he said. 'And do you know what? None of them know you're afraid to dance.'

'You're right,' she said, not looking at all convinced.

But when the MC invited the bridesmaid and grooms-man to get up onto the dance floor, Kate let him pull her to her feet. She was a little shaky but Sam didn't think anyone but he noticed it. He took her by the hand and led her onto the dance floor. She rested one hand on his shoulder and the other around his waist. Only he could feel her shivers of nervousness.

'Now we can shuffle,' he said. 'Just think of it like an ambulatory hug.'

'That's a Sam way of putting it,' she said, but she laughed. And he was glad he could make her laugh.

Kate had dreaded the dancing part of the evening. But standing there with Sam in the circle of his arms she felt safe, protected by his closeness. She trusted him not to let her make a fool of herself.

'I'm stepping my feet from side to side,' he said in an undertone she could only just hear over the music. 'We have to look like we're making an effort to dance. The people who know you're a professional dancer will be feeling sorry for you for being stuck with a shuffler grooms-man like me.'

Wrong! No woman in her right mind would ever pity her for being in Sam's arms. They'd envy her, more like it. She held on to him just a little bit tighter.

After the barefoot wedding ceremony, the bridal party had changed into high-heeled strappy sandals for the girls and loafers for the boys. She felt Sam's shoe nudge her toes.

'Hey, I felt that,' she said. 'Crushed toes aren't part of the deal.'

'I warned you I had two left feet.'

But she did as he suggested and stepped lightly from side to side. Securely held by Sam, as she tentatively started to move, the rhythm of the music seemed to invade her body. First her feet took off in something that was much more than a sideways shuffle, then her body started to sway. The old feeling came flooding back, the joy of her body moving—not just to the beat of the music but in step with Sam, who was also doing more than stepping from side to side.

Before she knew it, he had steered her into the centre of the dance floor and they were whirling around with the other couples. With a start of surprise, she realised she was being expertly led around the dance floor by a man who was light on his feet and perfectly in rhythm. She felt flushed with a relieved triumph that she had overcome her debilitating fear, and warm delight that she was back in the swing of things.

'I thought you said you couldn't dance,' she said to Sam.

'I said I had two left feet. But years of dancing instruction at my private boys' school beat a bit of coordination into them.'

'You had dance lessons at school?'

'It wasn't all rugby and cricket—though I was a far better football player than I ever was a dancer. We had to learn so we could dance with the girls from our corresponding girls' school. And take our place in Sydney society, of course.'

'I wish I'd known you when you were a schoolboy. I bet you were the hottest boy in your class.'

'I wouldn't say that,' he said, obviously uncomfortable

at such flattery—warranted though it was. She couldn't resist teasing him.

'I can imagine all the girls were after you.'

'Think again. I was this tall when I was thirteen. Big, awkward and shy.'

'I don't believe that for a moment.'

'Seriously. The other boys had way better chat-up lines than I did. By the time I'd thought about what I'd say, the girl had danced off with one of them.'

'Who needs chat-up lines when you're as handsome as you? Trust me, you would have been breaking girlish hearts all over the place. You could probably have had three at a time.'

'I hope not,' he said with genuine alarm. 'I'm a one-woman kind of guy.'

Suddenly the conversation had got kind of serious. And important.

'Really?' she said. Her breath caught in her throat.

'I met my first serious girlfriend in the final year of high school. She took a gap year in Europe and we broke up. Then there was a girl I dated at university and then Frances after that.'

'You…you don't have to give me your dating résumé,' she assured him.

'I want you to know you can trust me,' he said. Those bitter-chocolate-dark eyes searched hers.

'I think…I already know that,' she said.

'Good,' he replied and expertly twirled her around the floor until she was exhilarated and laughing. She couldn't remember when she'd enjoyed herself more.

Kate had been dancing for so long the soles of her feet were beginning to burn. All evening she'd regretted she hadn't worn her new shoes in—but then she hadn't anticipated she'd dance every dance. When the band took a break, she was hot and breathless and fanning herself with her hands.

'Some fresh air?' asked Sam.

'Absolutely,' she said, panting a little.

She followed Sam out onto the balcony away from the stuffiness and high chatter levels of the ball room. They virtually had the balcony to themselves, with only one other couple right down the other end.

The full moon reflected on the water of the bay. She took a deep breath of the cool night air. Sam leaned on the railing and looked out to sea. She slid her arms around his waist and rested her cheek against his broad back.

'Thank you for your help back there,' she murmured. 'I can't tell you how it feels to be able to dance again. I wouldn't have dared get up without you. Well, I might have, but maybe not for a long time and maybe—'

He turned around to face her. '*You* did it. Not me. But I'm happy I was able to help. Do you think, now you've danced once, you'll be able to do it again?'

She looked up at him. 'To be honest, I doubt I'll ever again dress up in a white leotard and bark like a poodle.'

He laughed. 'Sorry, but I wish I'd seen you. Do you have any photos?'

'*No.* And, if I did, no one would ever see them. It was hardly the highlight of my career as a professional dancer. A career I won't be reviving any time soon. But now it's not because I *can't,* but because I don't want to.'

'Sounds good to me.'

'It gives me hope I'll be able to get out of Dolphin Bay, too. I finally told Mum some of what happened in Sydney. She gave me the name of a psychologist at the hospital—someone I can speak to in confidence. I've made an appointment to see her next week.'

'That's a step in the right direction,' he said. 'I'm proud

of you. I know how difficult it's been for you to talk about it.'

'It's a small step. You're the one who can take the credit for helping me to get me this far.'

'I was just the shoulder you needed—'

'You were so, so much more than that, Sam.' She reached up and traced a line down his cheek with her fingers. Already his beard was growing and was rough under her fingertips. 'I…I hope I might be able to come and see you in Sydney before too long.'

He caught her hand and briefly pressed his lips to it. 'I wish you could come with me tomorrow.'

Joy bubbled through her that he should suggest it when deep down, in spite of her growing trust in him, she'd feared these few days might be all they'd ever have.

'Me too,' she said with a catch in her voice. 'But I can't. Not just because of…because of the dome but also because I'm looking after the hotel for the next ten days while Ben is on his honeymoon.'

'And helping out at Bay Books in your—' he made quotation marks with his fingers '—spare time.'

'It…it won't give me any time to mope around missing you,' she murmured, turning her head away, not wanting him to see the truth of how deeply she felt about him in her eyes.

With his index finger, he gently turned her chin back so she faced him. 'I'll miss you too,' he said. 'If I didn't have to go back to Sydney tomorrow morning, I wouldn't. But you know it's decision time at the meeting on Monday.'

'I know,' she said. 'I have every faith in you to make the right choice.'

His dark brows slanted. 'What happens if you don't get out from under that dome? If I sold the company, I could live anywhere I wanted. Even here.'

'In Dolphin Bay?' She shook her head. 'I don't think so.'

He cleared his throat. 'What I'm trying to say is that I want to spend more time with you, Kate. If that means moving to Dolphin Bay...'

She could hardly believe what she was hearing. 'I couldn't—wouldn't—ask that of you. You'd hate it here.'

'How can you be so sure of that?' he said. 'It...it's kind of growing on me. The community. The beach. The—'

'The way you'd be bored out of your brain within weeks?'

'I couldn't imagine ever being bored with you,' he said.

'Oh,' was all she managed to choke out in response.

He cradled her face in his two large, warm hands. His deep, brown eyes searched her face. 'Kate, in such a short time you...you've become...important to me.' Behind the imposing adult, the man who was gearing up to do battle in the boardroom over a multi-million-dollar deal, she saw the schoolboy, uncertain of the words he needed to find to win the girl.

'Oh, Sam, you've become so important to me too. But I...I... Until I get myself together I...'

He silenced her protest with a kiss. After a moment's surprised hesitation, she kissed him back and she gave herself up to the sheer pleasure of the pressure of his mouth on hers. Her lips parted on a sigh of bliss and his tongue slipped between them to tease and stroke and thrill. Her breath quickened. She met his tongue with hers and she pulled his head closer, her hands fisting in his hair. His hands slid down to her waist and drew her closer to his hard, muscular body. She could feel the frantic thudding of his heart, answered by the pounding of her own.

As the kiss flamed into something deeper and more passionate, desire ignited in delicious flames of want that surged through her, her breath coming hard and fast and broken. Sam groaned against her mouth and she answered the sensual sound by straining her body tighter to his.

She wanted him desperately—so desperately, she forgot she was on a balcony in close proximity to family and friends. Every sense was overwhelmed by her awakened need for him, the utter pleasure coursing through her body. Making her want more, making her want him at any cost.

She stilled. Her heart pounded harder, now from fear rather than passion as she realised the direction her thoughts had taken. This hunger for him would have her do anything he wanted. It could have her enslaved. It might transport her on a tide of need to an obsession where she lost all sense of herself. She felt like she was choking.

She wrenched away from Sam's arms and staggered backwards. He put out a hand to steady her. 'I…I can't do this,' she said.

He dropped his hand from her arm. His jaw clenched and his dark scowl was back, overlaid with both disbelief and pain.

'Because people can see us?' he growled. 'Because *Jesse* might see us?'

She shook her head. 'Because I want you so much and… it scares me.'

'This is about the guy at university,' he said flatly.

Mutely, she nodded.

His expression was grim as he seemed to gather his thoughts. Her heart sank to somewhere below her shoes. Had she scared him off with her endless fears?

'Kate, do you realise that this might scare me too? I've only known you a week and you're all I can think about. My feelings for you have become an issue in the most important decision I've ever had to make. This…this is new to me. I've laid it on the line for you. But are you ever going to be able to trust me?' He turned so his shoulder was facing her and his face was shrouded by shadow. Terror grabbed at her with icy claws.

He could walk away.

And that would be worse than anything else that could happen.

'Sam, I'm sorry. I…I've been so caught up in me and how I'm feeling, I…I didn't think enough about how it was affecting you.'

To her intense relief, he turned back so she could see his face, illuminated by the pale moonlight. 'I wouldn't break your spirit in the way that guy did. Your feistiness and independence are part of your appeal for me. I'm strong, Kate. I want to be there for you. You need time to sort through your issues and I know that. But it has to be two-way.'

She needed time. But it had been years since she'd fallen into that dark tunnel. Years when she'd hidden herself away, protecting herself against any real relationships by her fixation on Jesse, letting fear inhibit and stultify her emotional growth. She'd been a girl then, now she was a woman. She had to grow up. She had to come to Sam as an adult who considered his emotional needs as well as her own. Be aware that *she* could hurt *him*.

'Sam.' Urgently, she gripped his upper arms to keep him with her. She looked up into his eyes and her heart twisted painfully at the wariness that clouded them. No way could she lose him. 'You're right; I've been so focused on myself. I want a partnership. Me looking after you, as well as you looking after me. My shoulders aren't nearly as broad as yours, but I want them to be there for you like yours are for me.'

He started to say something but she rose up on her toes and silenced him with a kiss. She murmured against his mouth, 'And I want you. Tonight, when the party is over, I want to come with you to your room.'

He pulled back. She could see it was an effort for him but he managed a lopsided imitation of his usual wide grin. 'I want you too, believe me. I can't tell you how tempted I am to pick you up and carry you up to my room right now. But it wouldn't be right. It's too soon. And the whole of Dolphin Bay will know you've stayed with me. Neither of us wants that, especially as I'm going in the morning.'

Her body was still warm with want for him. But, in a way, she was relieved. It *was* too soon. The growing up she needed to do wasn't going to happen overnight. 'Yes. You're right.' But she twined her arms around his neck and drew him down for another kiss. 'But making love with you isn't an easy thing to say no to,' she murmured as she kissed him again.

'Woo-hoo!' Lizzie's voice interrupted them.

Kate pulled away from the kiss, flushed, her breathing erratic. Not only Lizzie, but also Jesse was standing in the doorway. Jesse caught her eye and winked. She knew Jesse so well, she realised that meant he approved of her and Sam getting together. What really surprised her was the knowing look Lizzie sent to Sam and the sheepish smile he sent her in return. What was that about?

'C'mon, you two, Sandy's about to toss her bouquet,' said Lizzie, ushering her and Sam back into the room. 'I'm staying right out of range but you, Kate, might want to be within catching distance.'

Did she?

After the encounter she'd just shared with Sam, was it weird to entertain the thought of marriage for even the briefest moments of wedding-fuelled madness? The groom in her 'walking to the altar' fantasy was tall, dark-haired and with a scowl that transformed into the sexiest of smiles…

For all they'd come to tonight, there was still much

both she and Sam needed to consider before she got carried away by dreams. Even if she did break her way free from the dome, what happened next?

Still, she had to admit to a twinge of disappointment when Sandy's bouquet went sailing over her, and the outstretched arms of all the other single ladies vying to catch it, to land fairly and squarely in Emily's lap. Kate was surprised by Emily's blushes and protests at the chants of, 'You're next,' 'Emily is next.' Hmm. She might have to quiz her little sister on the reason for those blushes.

But she forgot all about that as Sam put his arm around her to lead her over to the table that was serving coffee and slices of chocolate wedding cake.

'I hate fruit cake,' he said, picking up the biggest piece on the platter. 'When I get married, I'll want a chocolate cake.'

He said it so casually, seemingly without even being aware of the significance of his words, it made her wonder if Sam had a few dreams of his own.

CHAPTER TWELVE

SAM WOKE UP and for a long moment wasn't sure where he was. Then he realised he was sprawled across the sofa in Kate's living room. Kate was asleep, snuggled into his side, her head resting on his chest, her sweetly scented hair spilling over his neck. She was breathing deeply and evenly.

There were sooty smudges around her eyes where her make-up had smeared. Her lips were free of lipstick—it had been thoroughly kissed away. Her bridesmaid dress was rumpled up over her slender thighs. She'd kicked off her sandals and he noticed her toenails were painted the same pretty colour as her dress. He was fascinated by how pale her skin was, how he could see the delicate traceries of veins. Such a contrast to his own olive skin.

With her colouring, she certainly hadn't been made to live by the sea where so much activity was played out on the water or the sand under the blazing Australian sun. She loved her home town, but he suspected she was a city girl at heart. He thought she'd be happy in Sydney.

His Sydney was very different from the student haunts where she'd played out the relationship that had so traumatised her. The waterfront penthouse apartment he owned was part of a redeveloped wharf complex and was right next to some of the best restaurants in town. It was only a walk into the centre of the city. He reckoned she'd love it.

His arm was around her shoulder and he cautiously adjusted it to make himself more comfortable. She made a little murmur of protest deep in her throat and nestled in tighter, one hand clutching on to his chest. He dropped a light kiss on the top of her head.

He knew he should go, but he could not resist a few more moments of having her so close to him.

After the bride and groom had left the reception last night, he and Kate, along with Jesse, Lizzie and a group of their other friends, had adjourned to the bar at the Harbourside. Eventually it had ended up with just Kate and him left. There'd been nothing he wanted more than to take her up to his room and make love to her. But he had known, much as he'd wanted her, that wasn't going to happen. That *mustn't* happen. Instead he'd taken her home, she'd invited him in for coffee and they'd made out like teenagers on the sofa until they must have fallen asleep.

Sam smiled as he remembered how they'd kept talking until the time between each other's responses had got longer and longer until finally there had been silence. He hadn't wanted to let her go, hadn't wanted to say goodnight. And he didn't want to now.

The pale light of dawn was starting to filter through the blinds. He couldn't stay any longer. Not only would it be awkward for Dawn and Emily to come in and find him there, but he had to get on the road.

He edged his way into a sitting position and pulled Kate upright. He stroked her hair. 'Kate,' he whispered. 'I have to go.'

Her eyes opened, then shut again, then finally opened wide. She blinked as her eyes came into focus. 'Sam! Wh-where…? Oh. I remember now.' She stretched her arms languorously above her head, which made the top of her breasts swell over the edge of her strapless dress. She put her hand over her mouth as she yawned.

He averted his eyes to look over her head. Waking up with her pressed so intimately close was bad enough; seeing her skirt all rucked up around her thighs and the top starting to slide right off was more than a man could be expected to endure.

'C'mon, Kate.'

She planted her arms around his neck and pouted. 'No. Don't want you to go.' Her hair was all tousled and the smudged make-up around her eyes gave her a sultry air. The effect was adorable. She kissed him, her mouth soft and yielding, her tongue teasing the seam of his lips.

He groaned softly and kissed her back. Then he summoned every ounce of self-discipline he had to push himself up from the sofa, which in turn tipped her back against the cushions. She still looked groggy, a little bewildered and quite possibly half-asleep. Leaving her there was one of the most difficult things he had ever done.

He slipped into his shoes and picked up his car keys from the coffee table. Then he crouched down to the level of the sofa. 'Kate, listen. I'm leaving for Sydney as soon as I pick up my bag from the hotel. Do you understand?'

Her eyes widened and she nodded. 'Yes.' She pulled a sad, funny Kate face. 'I don't know when I'll next see you, but I hope it will be soon.'

'Me too,' he said. He kissed her gently on the mouth. 'Bye, Kate. You try to get some more sleep.'

''Kay,' she murmured.

He pulled a throw over her and tucked it around her bare legs. Then he let himself out of the door. He suspected she was asleep again before the door had closed behind him.

He forced his brain to change gears from thinking about making love to Kate to corporate responsibility and business pros and cons. And what would be the decision he would communicate to the potential purchaser of his company.

Her lingering perfume and the imprint of her body against his made his old workaholic tricks the least effective they'd ever been.

Kate had to put up with much teasing from her sister and mother when they discovered her dishevelled and asleep on the sofa, with two empty cups on the coffee table.

'I don't have to ask who you had here until all hours,' said Emily, her eyes dancing.

There was no point in denying it. Half of Dolphin Bay had probably seen her kissing Sam on the balcony of the hotel. And Emily had been among the group who'd congregated in the bar after the wedding reception. Kate and Sam had held hands the entire time.

As she showered, she thought that over breakfast might be a good time to talk through a few things with her mother and Emily.

The thought of their Sunday favourite of scrambled eggs and bacon made her gag. Not that she was feeling ill; it was just that her stomach was tied in knots of tension. She missed Sam already. It was devastating to think that when she started her shift at the hotel this afternoon he wouldn't be there. And she was also coming down from the high of all those frantic wedding preparations.

She waved away the eggs and instead nibbled on the platter of fruit Emily had cut up. Clearing up and doing the dishes was her breakfast task for today. As three adults sharing a house, they also shared the chores.

'So,' said her mother, sipping a cup of tea. 'Have you got something you want to say to us?'

'Something about someone?' said Emily. She broke into

the childish chant the sisters had used since they'd been tiny and still did. 'Someone whose name begins with *S?*'

Kate put down her own cup of herbal tea. 'Yes. I do. And it *is* about me and Sam.'

'Tell all,' said Emily, leaning forward on her elbows, her eyes avid.

'There's not a lot to tell yet, but there might be,' said Kate.

'We really like Sam, don't we, Mum?' asked Emily. Her mother nodded.

'I like him, too,' confessed Kate, the accursed blush betraying her. 'But he lives in Sydney and I live here. Which could be a problem.'

'Sweetie, there is that major issue for you to overcome before you can think about going to Sydney,' said her mum, raising her eyebrows in the direction of Emily. 'You know…'

'Don't worry, Mum, I've told Emily about the dome,' Kate said. She'd found visualising her issue as 'the dome' made it easier somehow to imagine herself breaking out of it. She wondered if the psychologist she was seeing on Tuesday would think it was a good idea.

'Good,' said her mother.

Kate took a deep breath. 'But there's another problem— one that doesn't just involve me. When I'm able to, I'll want to drive to Sydney fairly often. Who knows, I might end up living there one day before too long so I can date Sam, if I can afford exorbitant city rents. But…but I know I'm needed here. With you two.'

Her mother and Emily exchanged glances that Kate couldn't quite read.

She hastened to reassure them. 'Don't worry. If you want me to stay, we can work things out and—'

'Don't even *think* of giving up Sam for my sake,' said

Emily. 'A guy like him only comes along once in a million years. Grab on to him and don't let him go.'

'Er, Emily, that's not quite the way to put it,' said her mother. 'But we know what you mean and I echo the sentiment.'

Dawn reached out to give Kate a comforting pat on her arm. 'Don't worry about us, sweetie. It's been wonderful having you here with us all these years, and don't think I don't appreciate it. But things change. For all of us. You need to get your wings back and start to fly.'

'Actually, I have something to say too, Kate,' ventured Emily, an edge of excitement to her voice. 'I'm moving out next month. I didn't want to announce anything until it was certain. I've only just told Mum.'

Emily had talked about moving out on her own often enough but it was a big step. Kate was disconcerted it was actually happening. 'Where are you moving to?'

'To Melbourne. I'm going to share with some other basketball players in a house that's set up for wheelies. The bank has organised a transfer for me to a branch down there. I'm all set.'

Kate narrowed her eyes. 'And are all your new roomies female?'

'Um, no,' said Emily. 'But that's all very new and I don't want to jinx it by talking about him.'

'Okay,' said Kate, determined she would get all the details out of her sister before the end of the day. 'I'm really pleased for you. And visiting you will give me a good excuse to get to Melbourne.' Another reason to get out from under that dome.

She could feel her major tie to Dolphin Bay stretching and snapping. Emily didn't need her any more—though, if she was honest with herself, Emily hadn't needed her for a long time. *Had she needed to be needed?*

'So that just leaves you and me, Mum,' Kate said.

'I'm not pushing you out, Kate, but it will do you good to go when you're ready. I never imagined I'd have my great big girls of twenty-eight and twenty-six still living at home with me. It's time for me to have my independence too.'

Kate had inherited her tendency to blush from her mother and she was surprised at the rising colour on her mother's cheeks.

'I didn't know Colin's other name was "independence", Mum,' teased Emily.

Kate looked from her mother to Emily and back again. 'Colin?'

'My friend from the hospital—he's new in the admin department. He was the one who helped me and Sam put up the wedding arch. He…he's very nice.'

'And why didn't I know this?' demanded Kate.

'You're losing the plot, sister dear,' replied Emily. 'Too caught up with handsome Sam to keep your finger on the pulse of everyone else's business as you usually do.'

'And the wedding planning. And the resort stuff…' began Kate, and realised she was being overly defensive. She laughed. Maybe she didn't need to keep such a rigid control on things any more. Maybe there were fewer fears to keep at bay.

She'd ask Sam what he thought.

CHAPTER THIRTEEN

ON MONDAY MORNING, Sam sat behind the imposing desk that had once been his grandfather's in his office at the Sydney headquarters of Lancaster & Son Construction. He was aware if he went ahead with the sale of the family company that the name Lancaster & Son, founded by his grandfather, carried on by his father and then nurtured by him, would disappear into the history books.

That would be inevitable. But if he didn't have a son—or had a son who didn't want to go into the construction industry—would the name be such a loss?

In many ways it would be a relief—the burden of living up to that name and to his father's expectations would be finally lifted. He remembered back to the day he'd turned twenty-one when he'd demanded some autonomy from his father. Grudgingly, it had been given. But, even though his father had gone, there was still that feeling of having stepped into his shoes without having forged shoes of his own. He'd worked for the company since he'd been fourteen years old. Surely he deserved the chance for some cashed-up freedom?

Still, it was gut-wrenching to think of pulling the plug on so much of his family's endeavours. Thanks to his canny management, the company had been successful through all the ups and downs of the market. The balance sheet was very healthy with profits consistently rising—which was what made it so attractive to the company wanting to buy it. And the Lancaster reputation for quality and reliability was unsurpassed.

The money the sale would earn him was a mind-boggling amount, more than enough for him to start a business that was just his own. As well as the luxury of time to decide what that new venture might be.

It was a compelling reason to sell.

Again he flipped through the document that answered his questions about what the multi-national company intended to do if he accepted their offer. With the turn of each page, his gut clenched into tighter and more painful knots. Whatever labels you put on a business strategy, be they 'process re-engineering', 'shifting paradigms' or 'amalgamating cost centres', the truth of the matter was that the sale would result in downsizing. And not one member of his crew deserved to lose their job. There were the clients to consider too—clients who trusted him. Clients like his friend Ben Morgan.

He thought about what Kate had said—and knew there was much truth in her words. With his inheritance had come responsibilities. His father had been fond of that old-fashioned word 'duty'. In the contemporary world of dog-eat-dog business, did words like 'responsibility' and 'duty' have a place—or were they just remnants of a more honourable past?

Then there was his personal life to consider. His workaholic devotion to the company had lost him a fiancée. Now he'd fallen for a woman who might not be able to leave her small, coastal home town in the short-term; perhaps not for a long time. If he wanted to be with her, he might have to live there too. What had she said? *You'd be bored out of your brain within weeks.*

He'd started to be seduced by Dolphin Bay but now he was back in Sydney the thought of living in a backwater became less and less appealing. Even with Kate by his side, a ton of money in the bank and freedom from corporate responsibility, he suspected he would find it stifling.

If he took that path, might he come to resent her? Might that resentment become a poison that would destroy their relationship before it would have time to flourish?

There was such a short time left for him to make his momentous decision. He leaned back in his big leather chair, linked his hands behind his head, closed his eyes and reviewed again his options.

It seemed like no time at all had elapsed before his PA buzzed him that his meeting was about to start.

He picked up the folder with all the relevant documents and headed for the boardroom.

Kate was on edge all morning. From the time Sam's meeting was scheduled, she had started checking her mobile phone for messages. Whatever decision he made it would be life-changing for him—and possibly for her.

When the call finally came, she found her hands were shaking as she picked up her phone. 'Well?' she asked him. She held her breath for his answer.

'I didn't sell,' he said. 'The company is still mine.'

She let out her breath in a sigh. 'Congratulations. I'm proud of you. It must have been difficult but I think you made the right decision.'

'Me too. I did that "make a choice and live with it for an hour" exercise—and decided to sell. But as I headed to the meeting, and realised it would be the last time I would have a say in the business, I knew there was nothing I'd rather do than run Lancaster & Son Construction. I finally understood that my inheritance had never been a burden but a privilege. And that it was entirely up to me how I chose to direct it—my vision, my future. So I changed my mind.'

'Which means everyone gets to keep their jobs and Ben gets to keep his builder.'

'All that.'

'I'd like to give you a big hug.'

'A big Kate hug is just what I need right now. I didn't realise just how stressful the whole process would be.' She could sense the weariness in his voice.

'I wish I…'

'You wish what?'

'Oh, I wish I could hop in the car and drive up to Sydney to be with you to celebrate. But obviously that can't be.'

'You'll get there, just give it time,' he said. It still amazed her that this big, sexy hunk of a man could be so considerate.

She took another deep breath. 'I've got a new goal to aim for—besides seeing the Indian palace hotel, that is. When Ben comes back from his honeymoon, I plan to drive up to Sydney to see you.'

There was silence at the other end of the line. 'You're sure that's not too ambitious?'

She shook her head, even knowing he couldn't see her. 'No. I'm going to drive a little further every day until I can point that car in the direction of Sydney and go for it. And hope I don't drive smack into the dome, of course.'

'Okay. But don't beat yourself up about it if the practice proves more difficult than the theory.'

'I won't,' she promised.

There was a pause on the line before Sam spoke again. 'Unfortunately, the decision to hold on to the company means it's unlikely I'll make it down to Dolphin Bay. Not before the time Ben gets back, anyway.'

Disappointment, dark and choking, constricted her

voice but she forced herself to sound cheerful. 'That's okay. I'll...I'll be so flat out with everything here. Not to mention the daily get-out-of-town driving goals I've set myself that—'

'It's not okay,' he said. 'But because I've been away for a week, and because I've got to be seen to be taking the reins with confidence, that's the way it's got to be. There are changes I want to make straight away. This is seen as a turning point for the company.' She suspected his words were accompanied by a shrug. 'I'm sorry,' he added.

Her voice was too choked to reply immediately and she nodded. But of course he couldn't see that. She donned her 'everything is just fine' voice. 'Sure. We can call or text. Maybe even video calls.'

'It won't be the same as seeing you but, yes, that's what we'll do. Now, I have to go for the first of a long line-up of meetings. The start of the new era.'

'Where the company is truly yours—in your mind, anyway.'

There was silence at the end of the line and Kate thought he might have hung up. But he spoke again. 'You're very perceptive. That's exactly what the decision has meant to me.'

When Kate put down the phone she was more than ever determined to get out of that dome so she could take more control of her life—and choose when she wanted to see Sam, rather than waiting for him to come to her.

By Wednesday afternoon, Kate had driven further away from Dolphin Bay town centre than she had for two years. While being aware there was such a thing as overconfidence, she felt buoyed by the knowledge that she had got into the car without shaking or nausea. By the end of the ten days, she was sure she would make it onto the Princes Highway and away.

The initial meeting with the psychologist had gone well. She'd been surprised that the thoughtful, middle-aged woman hadn't wanted to talk much about the past. Rather, she'd acknowledged that Kate—thanks to her talks with Sam—already had a level of insight into what had caused her problems. Then the psychologist had gone straight into examining and challenging Kate's thoughts and feelings. At the second session on Wednesday morning, she'd given her strategies for coping in trigger situations, like getting into cars. Kate had found the breathing techniques and visualisations particularly helpful.

She'd been amazed that she could progress so quickly when she'd thought it might take months—even years— to get to the bottom of things. Why on earth hadn't she admitted to herself long ago that she'd needed help, when the solution seemed so straightforward?

By the following Tuesday, on her morning off, she drove all the way south to the larger town of Bateman's Bay nearly an hour away. She strolled up and down the water-front, revelling in her freedom. Then she sat in a café right on the water and congratulated herself for having pushed the boundary of the dome so far back. She was confident that by Friday she'd be on the road north to Sydney, count-ing down the minutes until she saw Sam.

After she finished her coffee, she decided to phone Sam on her mobile to share the good news. She'd be in Sydney on Friday in time to meet him for dinner.

'I'm so proud of you, you're doing amazingly well,' he said. 'But there's going to be a change of plan.'

Kate swallowed hard against that same lump of disap-pointment that seemed to rise in her throat when she talked to Sam about her plans to visit him in Sydney. But she refused to listen to the nagging, internal voice that taunted her that she had, once again, been a bad judge of a man's character. That maybe, just maybe, Sam would hedge and defer and change dates until it ended up that she would never see him again.

Trust him, trust him, trust him, she chanted to herself.

'A change of plan?' she repeated, desperately fighting a dull edge to her voice.

'Not such a bad one,' he said. 'At least, I don't think you'll find it so bad. In fact, I'm sure you'll think it's good news.' There was a rising tone of restrained excitement to his voice that made her wonder.

'Okay, so enough with the torture,' she said. 'Tell me what it is.'

'I have to fly to Singapore tonight for a series of meetings that will go on until the weekend.'

'And that's good news?' she said, her heart sinking.

'The good news is I want you to meet me there. Now that you've told me you'll be in Sydney, I'm confident you can do it. I'll send you an email with the details.'

She had to pause to get her thoughts together. 'In Singapore? You want me to meet you in Singapore?' She wasn't sure if the churning in her stomach was dread or excitement.

'Yes.'

'When I've only just managed Bateman's Bay?'

'You can do it, Kate. I know you can. Especially when you hear where we'll be staying in Singapore. Remember the hotel you told me about that shared top spot with the Indian palace one on your list of must-see hotels?'

'The huge new one with the mammoth towers and the world's highest infinity pool, fifty-seven floors up?'

'The very one.'

'The one with the amazing spa on the fifty-fifth floor?'

'Yup,' he confirmed.

'And the luxury shopping mall underneath, and the casino, and what they say are the best views in Singapore?' By now she was practically screeching with excitement. A couple at the next table looked at her oddly and she lowered her voice.

'I've booked a suite on the highest floor I could,' he said. 'With a butler.'

'A butler? You're kidding me.'

'No. Nothing short of the lap of luxury for Ms Parker.'

'But...but you'll already be there and I'll have to get there by myself. I don't know that I—'

'If you can get to Sydney, all you have to do is get to the airport. There'll be a first-class ticket waiting for you. You'll hardly know you're in the air.'

She lowered her voice to a note above a whisper. 'But, Sam, what if I can't do it? What if I don't get as far as Sydney?'

'Then we cancel it all and wait until I can get down there to see you.'

'Okay. So I have an escape route.'

'If you like to see it as that, yes,' he said. 'But Kate, here's the deal: to make it easier for you, I'll send down a chauffeur-driven limo to pick you up from home. He'll drive you to Sydney International Airport so you don't actually have to worry about driving. That will be one less pressure on you. The driver—who is on my staff—will escort you into the first-class lounge where you can check in. Then I'll meet you at the other end.'

'Sam, I so want to see you. I...I miss you. And this all sounds terribly exciting. Like a dream, really.'

'So you'll do it?'

'Just give me a second.' She took a few of the controlled, calming breaths she had been practising. 'Yes. I'll do it.

Mum told me I needed to get my wings back but I didn't know that she meant aeroplane wings.'

'Great,' he said and she was surprised at the relief in his voice.'

'Sam?' she ventured. 'Thank you. This might just be the incentive I need to get me out of that dome once and for all. I'll see you in Singapore.'

CHAPTER FOURTEEN

I CAN DO THIS. Kate kept repeating the words like a mantra as the ultra-smooth limousine, way too big for one person, left Dolphin Bay behind. She realised she was sitting rigidly on the edge of the seat and she made herself sink back into its well-upholstered comfort.

She'd only had a light breakfast, but felt a little queasy, so she made herself take the controlled, calming breaths the psychologist had taught her. Buried deep in her hand-bag was some prescription medication she'd got from her doctor, as insurance in case she got overwhelmed by panic. But she was determined it would not come out of its wrapping. She wanted to be with Sam. To be with Sam, she had to stay in this car and not beg the driver to take her home. She was determined to find the strength to turn her life around. *I can do this.*

She pulled out her phone from her bag and flicked through to the photos of the wedding. There was a lovely one of Sam and her, she smiling up at him, him with his dark head bent to hear what she was saying. She pressed a kiss to her finger and transferred the kiss to the photo. All this was worth it.

It didn't seem long before coastal bushland made way for rolling green farmland. She gazed out the window and marvelled that she had not been along these roads for five years. But that self-imposed isolation was behind her now. She'd smashed through the dome.

The previous night she'd had a broken sleep, kept awake by alternate bouts of churning excitement and worry. Three times she'd got out of bed to check that her passport and travel documents were packed. By the time the car was driving through the picturesque town of Berry, she was fast asleep.

The driver woke her as they approached Sydney International Airport. She looked around her, bewildered, until she realised where she was. A wave of exultation surged through her. *I've done it!*

The last time she'd flown, it had been with the dance troupe. That had involved a bus ride to the airport and the cheapest of bargain airline seats right down the back of the plane.

Being ushered into the first-class lounge was a different experience altogether. She tried not to look too awestruck at the level of elegant luxury that surrounded her. Customers waiting for their flights could enjoy anything from a snack to a three-course meal. There was even a day spa where she could book in for a facial—all part of the service. It was like a six-star hotel on a smaller scale. But she couldn't enjoy it—even if she tried looking on it as research.

Everyone else seemed to know where they were going, what they were doing. The staff bustled around, greeting frequent flyers by name but not paying her any attention. Kate felt awkward and alone and unable to pretend she fitted in. She sat huddled on the edge of an ultra-contemporary leather sofa with a plate of gourmet snacks uneaten on the small table beside her.

She was wearing slim black trousers, a silk tank top and a loose, fine-knit black jacket trimmed with bronze metallic studs. Teamed with black ballet flats, she thought her outfit looked fine and would be comfortable for the flight.

But there wasn't a designer-label attached to any of it.

And this was designer label territory.

Was this Sam's world? She hadn't thought of him being super-wealthy but the personal chauffeur and the first-class travel indicated otherwise.

How well did she actually know him?

Every so often, boarding calls went out over the sound system. Each time she thought it might be for her. Each time she realised she'd forgotten her flight number and had to fumble in her bag to pull out her boarding card. Each time she got more and more flustered.

She began to dread the thought of actually boarding the plane—seven hours cooped up with no possibility of escape. Seven hours of escalating worry. What if Sam wasn't there to meet her at the other end? What if she had to find her own way to the hotel in a foreign city? What if she got lost?

Dread percolated in the pit of her belly. She started to shake and tried to control it by wringing her hands together. Her heart thudded wildly. Perspiration prickled on her forehead. *She couldn't do this.*

She used her breathing techniques to slow down the panic—then started to feel angry. This wasn't about an unresolved issue in her past. It was about Sam.

Sam should not have expected this of her. This was forcing her to run before she was even sure she could walk. He knew her problems only too well—and she'd thought he understood them. She should not be expected to fly to Singapore on her own. This was the first time she had been able to venture out of her home town for five years. To pop her on a plane all by herself like a first-class parcel and expect her to cope was nothing short of cruel.

It dawned on her that, not only hadn't she seen Sam since he'd gone back to Sydney, she hadn't really talked to him that much either. He was always preoccupied with the company he had taken charge of with renewed vigour. What had he said about the reason for his cancelled wedding? *I was a selfish workaholic.*

Obviously things hadn't changed. *He* hadn't changed.

Maybe Sam in Dolphin Bay and Sam in Sydney were two different people. Away from stress and the pressure of his job, he'd been the kind, thoughtful man she'd fallen in love with. But back on the city treadmill he'd become that ruthless, selfish person she'd always suspected might be there beneath the surface—a man whose woman would always come second to his business, who would have to fit in around him when it suited him.

She didn't want that kind of man.

It had been a classic holiday romance, she supposed with a painful lurch of her heart. Only he had been the one on holiday and she had been the one left behind when he'd gone home. He had been more than generous with dollars in organising this trip for her. But he had been exceedingly stingy with his time.

Sure, she'd wanted to see that wonderful hotel in Singapore. But most of all she'd wanted to see *him.* Now, on top of the shaking and shivering and cold sweats, she felt tears smarting. *She could not get on that plane.*

No way could she risk a public meltdown high in the sky somewhere between Sydney and Singapore. Only to be met at the other end —if he wasn't too busy in a business meeting—by someone she was no longer certain she wanted to see.

Kate swallowed the sob that threatened to break out, got up from the sofa and picked up her bag. She couldn't go home, that was for sure. Instead she'd march out to the taxi rank and get a ride to one of the glamorous new Sydney hotels she'd explored only on their websites. There she'd lock herself away for a few days, cry her eyes out, order room service and figure out where she went from there.

But as she headed towards the exit she was blocked by a tall, dark-haired man wearing a crumpled business suit, sporting dark stubble and an expression of anguish. 'Kate. Thank heaven. What was I thinking of, to expect you to fly by yourself?'

Her heart starting pounding so hard she had to put her hand to her chest. Sam. Gorgeous, wonderful, sexy Sam. She desperately wanted to throw herself into his arms. But that wouldn't work.

Kate looked at him with an expression of cold distaste in her beautiful green eyes. How could Sam blame her? He'd been nothing short of inept in the way he'd gone about this whole trip, a trip that was supposed to give her a treat and cement their relationship.

He could blame the pressures of the sale decision and subsequent reassurances to the staff, many of whom had been unsettled by the reports in the press about the potential takeover. But that was no real excuse.

By the time he'd finally got some time to himself on the plane to Singapore, he'd realised what he'd done. He'd reverted to the same old bad, work-obsessed ways that had destroyed his relationships before. After all that angst over the sale of the company, the new direction he wanted to take, he hadn't changed a bit. He'd expected a girl struggling to overcome a form of agoraphobia to do what must have seemed impossible to her. What kind of fool was he?

Kate went to move away from him and he realised she was heading towards the exit. 'Kate, where are you going? We have to board the plane in ten minutes.'

She spun back on her heel. '*We?* Sam, what are you doing here? I'm confused, to say the least.' He realised she was dangerously close to tears—tears caused by him. The knowledge stabbed him with pain and guilt for hurting her.

'I got to Singapore and realised what an idiot I was to expect you to get on a plane by yourself. So I got another plane back here as soon as I could so we could fly together.'

Her brow furrowed. 'You *what?*'

'I just flew back from Singapore. My plane landed here at this terminal. I wanted to be here to meet you when you arrived by limo, but the plane was late and there was a hellish crowd in the arrivals hall. Thankfully, I got here in time.' He would never have forgiven himself if he had missed her.

A smile struggled to melt her frosty expression. 'I don't believe what I'm hearing.'

'I booked another ticket for me so we could fly together, like we should have in the first place.'

'But what about your meetings in Singapore?'

'I rearranged them.'

'Weren't they important?' she asked.

'Nothing is more important than you, Kate.'

He didn't blame her for the scepticism that extinguished that nascent smile. He put his hands on her shoulders and this time she didn't move away. 'Seriously. I had a lot of time to think on that plane coming back to Sydney. I realised I had to change my obsessive, destructive, workaholic ways or I'd lose you. And I couldn't bear that.'

'So what do you intend to do?' she asked.

'Delegate. Give some of the really good people I have in my organisation more chance to manage. My father's old right-hand man has been seriously under-utilised because I saw him as a threat rather than a help. Most of all, I'm going to build in time for the woman I love.'

Her eyes widened with astonishment. 'Did…did you just say you…?'

'That I loved you? Yes, I did. And I'll say it again—I love you, Kate Parker.' He gathered her into his arms and kissed her on the mouth.

After the frantic dash from the plane to the lounge, Sam had been so engrossed with making sure Kate would be getting on the plane with him that he had completely forgotten about his surroundings. He was brought back to reality by a polite smattering of applause and turned around to see that they had attracted a smiling audience.

He looked at Kate and she blushed and laughed, her dimples flirting in her cheeks. She turned to face the people applauding and dipped a deep, theatrical, dancer's curtsey. He joined her in a half-bow of acknowledgement. Then he took her hand and tugged her towards him. 'C'mon, we've got a plane to catch.'

Travelling first class was an adventure all on its own, Kate thought as they disembarked in Singapore. She'd enjoyed a fully flat bed, pillows, blankets, luxury toiletries, even pyjamas. And the food had been top-class-restaurant standard delivered with superlative service.

The best thing of all had been Sam's company. After his frantic dash from Sydney to Singapore and back again, he'd drowsed for much of the flight, but every moment they'd both been awake they'd been together. She'd even managed to ask her final question, number five—how had he got that scar on his eyebrow? The prosaic answer related to an unfortunate encounter with a sharp metal window frame being moved around on a building site. She would have preferred something more romantic but, as he'd said in his practical way, he was lucky he hadn't lost an eye.

And now was her first sight of exotic Singapore.

Another limousine was there to pick them up. As she waited for her suitcase to be loaded into the boot, she sniffed the warm, humid air, tinged with a fragrance she didn't recognise. She asked Sam what it was.

'I call it the scent of Asia—a subtle mix of different plants, foods, spices. I find it exciting every time I smell it—and it's intoxicating when it's the first time.'

She couldn't agree more. *She was in Asia!*

It was night-time, and Singapore was a city sparkling with myriad fairy-tale lights that delighted her. As they drove across a bridge, her first sight of their hotel made her gasp. Brightly lit, its three tall towers seemed to rear up out of the water, the famous roof-top pool resort slung across the very top.

'I can't wait to get up there and swim on the top of the world,' she said. She clutched Sam's arm. 'Oh, thank you for bringing me here. This is the most amazing place I've ever seen.'

'I'm happy to be sharing it with you.' He smiled his slow, sexy smile. 'Around here is the really modern part of Singapore. Most of this area is built on reclaimed land—it's an engineering marvel. Tomorrow I'll take you to the old part. There's a mix of gracious buildings from the colonial past and temples I think you'll find fascinating.'

'I'll look forward to it,' she said. 'You know, I'm having to pinch myself to make sure this is all real and I'm not dreaming.'

He laughed. 'It's real, all right.' He looked down at her. 'But the best part is having you here with me.'

'Agreed,' she said happily, squeezing his hand.

Thank heaven, she thought, as she had thought a hundred times already, she hadn't walked out of that exit back at Sydney airport.

Inside, the hotel didn't disappoint. The atrium was so

mind-bogglingly spacious she got a sore neck from looking upwards. And the interior design was like nothing
she'd ever seen—upmarket contemporary, with Oriental
highlights that made it truly unique.

'Considering your interest in hotels, I've arranged for
you to have a private tour,' Sam said as they went up in
the elevator to their room. 'You just have to decide on a
time that suits you.'

'You've thought of everything,' she replied with a con-
tented sigh.

'Except the most important thing,' he said with a wry
twist to his mouth. 'I'll never forgive myself for expect-
ing you to get on that plane by yourself.'

Kate silenced him with a halt sign. 'I've forgiven you, so
you have to forgive yourself. Really. You realised your mistake and remedied it with the most marvellous of gestures.'

'So long as you're okay with it,' he said. 'I shocked
myself at how easily I relapsed into work-obsessed ways.'

'So, I'm going to police this workaholic thing,' she as-
serted more than half-seriously. 'It's not good for you. Or
me.'

'You can discipline me whenever you like,' he shot back
with a wicked lift of his eyebrow.

'Count on it,' she said, smiling as the elevator doors
opened on their floor.

The first thing she noticed when they walked into their
spacious suite wasn't the smart design or the view across
the harbour. It was the fact that in the open-plan bathroom
the elegant, free-standing bathtub was full of water and
had sweetly fragrant rose petals scattered across the surface. When she looked across to the bed, rose petals had
also been scattered across it.

'How romantic!' she exclaimed, clapping her hands in
delight. 'Did you organise this too?'

'I can't take the credit,' he said. 'The hotel staff…uh… they seemed to think we were on our honeymoon.'

'Oh,' she said. 'Well, I hope… That is, I'd like to think this will be a…a honeymoon of sorts.' She wound her arms around his neck. 'Sam, this hotel is wonderful. Singapore is wonderful. All the stuff you've got planned for us is wonderful. But just being alone with you is the most wonderful thing of all.'

She kissed him, loving his taste, the roughness of his beard, the hard strength of his body pressed close to hers. 'I'd have to argue that you're the most wonderful of the wonderful,' he murmured against her mouth.

'I've never been so lonely as those days in Dolphin Bay after you went home. I ached to be with you,' she confessed.

'One night, after a business dinner, I got into the car and decided to drive down just to see you for an hour or two,' he said.

'So why didn't you?'

'Because I figured I'd end up driving home at night without sleeping at all and thought there was a good chance I'd crash the car.'

She stilled as she thought of the accident that had injured Emily and ultimately, because of its repercussions, taken her father's life too. 'I'm so glad you stayed put,' she said. 'Although I probably wouldn't have let you go back if you'd come.'

He kissed her and she eagerly kissed him back. Then she broke away to plant hungry little kisses along the line of his jaw, and came back to claim his mouth again in a deep kiss that rapidly became urgent with desire.

Without breaking the kiss, he slid her jacket off her shoulders so it fell to the floor. She fumbled with his tie, and when it didn't come undone easily she broke away from the kiss with a murmur of frustration so she could see what she was doing.

'Did I tell you how incredibly sexy you look in a suit?' she asked, her breath coming rapidly as she pulled off his tie and started to unbutton his shirt so she could push her hands inside. His chest was rock-solid with muscle, his skin smooth and warm. 'But then you look incredibly sexy in jeans too. Maybe you look incredibly sexy in anything— or maybe nothing.'

Her body ached with want for him. And this time there was no reason to stop—except *he* stopped. 'Wait,' he said.

'I don't want to wait,' she urged breathlessly. 'We're in the honeymoon suite.'

He stepped back. 'Seriously. I have to tell you something,' he said, the words an effort through his laboured breathing.

'Okay,' she replied, thinking of the bed behind her and how soon she could manoeuvre him onto it.

'Kate, listen—I can see where this is heading.'

'Good,' she said.

'And I don't think you're ready for it.'

Her eyes widened. 'Let me be the judge—' she started to say.

'Please,' he broke in. 'This is important. I've told you before, I want you to be able to trust me.'

'Yes,' she said.

'I want you to be sure of me before we…we make love.'

She wasn't certain what he was trying to say but she sensed it was important. Very important.

'What I'm trying to say is that if we wait until we're married you'll have no doubts about how committed I am to you. And it will give you the security I think you really need.'

She stared at him, lost for words, but with a feeling of intense joy bubbling through her.

'I'm asking you to marry me, Kate,' he said hoarsely.

'And…and I'm saying yes,' she whispered.

He gathered her into his arms and hugged her close. They stood, arms wrapped around each other for a long moment, when all she was aware of was his warmth and strength, the thudding of his heart and their own ragged breathing.

'I love you, Sam,' she said. 'I…I couldn't say it at the airport in front of all those people. It's too…too private.'

'I didn't mean to say it there; no one was more surprised than I was. I was just so relieved you hadn't flown away already, never to speak to me again, when you discovered I wasn't in Singapore to meet you.'

Then and there, she resolved never to tell him that she'd been on her way out of the airport when he'd found her.

'There's another thing,' he said, reaching into his pocket and pulling out a little black velvet box. 'I want to make it official.'

She drew a sharp intake of breath. It couldn't be. *It just couldn't be.* That would be too, too perfect.

With a hand that wasn't quite steady, she took the box from him and opened it. Inside was an exquisite ring, set with a baguette-cut emerald surrounded by two baguette-cut diamonds. 'Sam. It's perfect.'

'I thought it went with the colour of your eyes,' he said, sounding very pleased with himself in a gruff, masculine way. 'There's a good jewellery shop in the shopping arcade attached to the hotel.'

'I love it,' she whispered as Sam slipped it on to the third finger of her left hand. 'I absolutely love it.' She held her hand up in front of her for them both to admire. 'It's a perfect fit.'

'Lucky guess,' he said. 'Though, we builders are good with measurements.'

'Clever you,' she said, kissing him.

'I'd like to get married as soon as possible,' he declared. 'So we can…?'

'Not just because of that. Because I want you to be my wife.'

'And I love the idea of you being my husband,' she murmured. 'My husband,' she repeated, liking the sound of the words.

'Obviously, with the business, there's no way I can live in Dolphin Bay—though we can buy a holiday house there if you like. We'll have to live in Sydney. If that's okay with you.'

'Yes,' she said. 'I'd like that. Though, there are things we need to sort out. Like Ben. My job.'

'I don't think Ben will be at all surprised to be losing you, and you'll still be involved with the new resort as a part owner.'

'And through my connection with the owner of the construction company,' she said.

'I was thinking of setting up a hotel development division in the business,' he told her. 'What do you think?'

'That I could work with?' she asked.

He nodded. 'Of course, that would involve necessary research visiting fabulous hotels all around the world with your husband.'

'That seems a sound business proposition,' she said.

'Starting with a certain palace hotel in India where we can have our real honeymoon.'

'And write it off on expenses,' she said with a giggle.

'I like your thinking,' he said. 'Welcome to Lancaster & Son Construction, Mrs Lancaster-To-Be.'

'We…we might have a son,' she said. 'The name would live on.'

'Or a daughter. Or both. I want at least two children, if that's okay by you. I hated being an only child.'

'Quite okay with me,' she said on a sigh of happiness.

She wound her arms around his neck, loving it when her ring flashed under the light. 'Sam? I feel like I really trust you now. And I'm very sure of your commitment.'

'Yes,' he murmured, kissing the soft hollow at the base of her throat.

'And I want you to be sure of my love and commitment.'

'Thank you,' he said.

'We're officially engaged now, aren't we? You're my fiancé, right?'

'Yes,' he replied, planting a trail of little kisses up her neck to the particularly sensitive spot under her ear. It was almost unbearably pleasurable.

'So do you think we could start our practice honeymoon now?'

She looked meaningfully across at the enormous bed, covered in pink rose petals.

'Good idea,' he said as he picked her up and carried her towards it.

* * * * *

Mills & Boon® Hardback
July 2014

ROMANCE

Christakis's Rebellious Wife	Lynne Graham
At No Man's Command	Melanie Milburne
Carrying the Sheikh's Heir	Lynn Raye Harris
Bound by the Italian's Contract	Janette Kenny
Dante's Unexpected Legacy	Catherine George
A Deal with Demakis	Tara Pammi
The Ultimate Playboy	Maya Blake
Socialite's Gamble	Michelle Conder
Her Hottest Summer Yet	Ally Blake
Who's Afraid of the Big Bad Boss?	Nina Harrington
If Only...	Tanya Wright
Only the Brave Try Ballet	Stefanie London
Her Irresistible Protector	Michelle Douglas
The Maverick Millionaire	Alison Roberts
The Return of the Rebel	Jennifer Faye
The Tycoon and the Wedding Planner	Kandy Shepherd
The Accidental Daddy	Meredith Webber
Pregnant with the Soldier's Son	Amy Ruttan

MEDICAL

200 Harley Street: The Shameless Maverick	Louisa George
200 Harley Street: The Tortured Hero	Amy Andrews
A Home for the Hot-Shot Doc	Dianne Drake
A Doctor's Confession	Dianne Drake

Mills & Boon® Large Print
July 2014

ROMANCE

A Prize Beyond Jewels	Carole Mortimer
A Queen for the Taking?	Kate Hewitt
Pretender to the Throne	Maisey Yates
An Exception to His Rule	Lindsay Armstrong
The Sheikh's Last Seduction	Jennie Lucas
Enthralled by Moretti	Cathy Williams
The Woman Sent to Tame Him	Victoria Parker
The Plus-One Agreement	Charlotte Phillips
Awakened By His Touch	Nikki Logan
Road Trip with the Eligible Bachelor	Michelle Douglas
Safe in the Tycoon's Arms	Jennifer Faye

HISTORICAL

The Fall of a Saint	Christine Merrill
At the Highwayman's Pleasure	Sarah Mallory
Mishap Marriage	Helen Dickson
Secrets at Court	Blythe Gifford
The Rebel Captain's Royalist Bride	Anne Herries

MEDICAL

Her Hard to Resist Husband	Tina Beckett
The Rebel Doc Who Stole Her Heart	Susan Carlisle
From Duty to Daddy	Sue MacKay
Changed by His Son's Smile	Robin Gianna
Mr Right All Along	Jennifer Taylor
Her Miracle Twins	Margaret Barker

Mills & Boon® Hardback

August 2014

ROMANCE

Zarif's Convenient Queen	Lynne Graham
Uncovering Her Nine Month Secret	Jennie Lucas
His Forbidden Diamond	Susan Stephens
Undone by the Sultan's Touch	Caitlin Crews
The Argentinian's Demand	Cathy Williams
Taming the Notorious Sicilian	Michelle Smart
The Ultimate Seduction	Dani Collins
Billionaire's Secret	Chantelle Shaw
The Heat of the Night	Amy Andrews
The Morning After the Night Before	Nikki Logan
Here Comes the Bridesmaid	Avril Tremayne
How to Bag a Billionaire	Nina Milne
The Rebel and the Heiress	Michelle Douglas
Not Just a Convenient Marriage	Lucy Gordon
A Groom Worth Waiting For	Sophie Pembroke
Crown Prince, Pregnant Bride	Kate Hardy
Daring to Date Her Boss	Joanna Neil
A Doctor to Heal Her Heart	Annie Claydon

MEDICAL

Tempted by Her Boss	Scarlet Wilson
His Girl From Nowhere	Tina Beckett
Falling For Dr Dimitriou	Anne Fraser
Return of Dr Irresistible	Amalie Berlin

Mills & Boon® Large Print

August 2014

ROMANCE

A D'Angelo Like No Other	Carole Mortimer
Seduced by the Sultan	Sharon Kendrick
When Christakos Meets His Match	Abby Green
The Purest of Diamonds?	Susan Stephens
Secrets of a Bollywood Marriage	Susanna Carr
What the Greek's Money Can't Buy	Maya Blake
The Last Prince of Dahaar	Tara Pammi
The Secret Ingredient	Nina Harrington
Stolen Kiss From a Prince	Teresa Carpenter
Behind the Film Star's Smile	Kate Hardy
The Return of Mrs Jones	Jessica Gilmore

HISTORICAL

Unlacing Lady Thea	Louise Allen
The Wedding Ring Quest	Carla Kelly
London's Most Wanted Rake	Bronwyn Scott
Scandal at Greystone Manor	Mary Nichols
Rescued from Ruin	Georgie Lee

MEDICAL

Tempted by Dr Morales	Carol Marinelli
The Accidental Romeo	Carol Marinelli
The Honourable Army Doc	Emily Forbes
A Doctor to Remember	Joanna Neil
Melting the Ice Queen's Heart	Amy Ruttan
Resisting Her Ex's Touch	Amber McKenzie

Discover more romance at

www.millsandboon.co.uk

- ❤ WIN great prizes in our exclusive competitions
- ❤ BUY new titles before they hit the shops
- ❤ BROWSE new books and REVIEW your favourites
- ❤ SAVE on new books with the Mills & Boon® Bookclub™
- ❤ DISCOVER new authors

PLUS, to chat about your favourite reads, get the latest news and find special offers:

- 📘 Find us on facebook.com/millsandboon
- 🐦 Follow us on twitter.com/millsandboonuk
- ❤ Sign up to our newsletter at millsandboon.co.uk